MARVEL ACTION
BLACK PANTHER
RISE TOGETHER

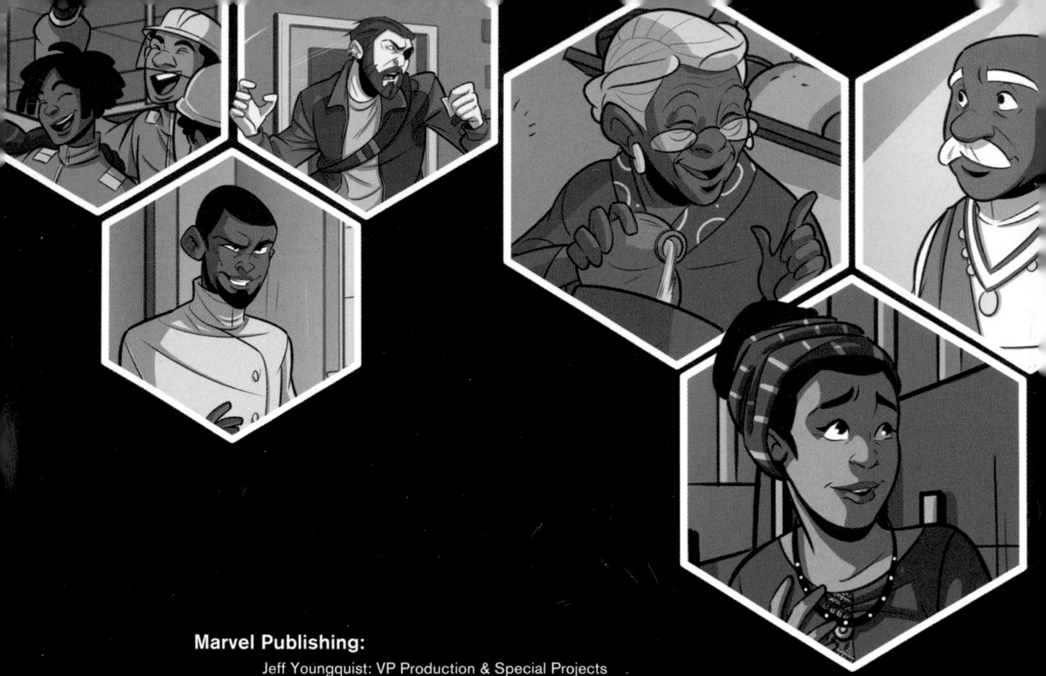

Marvel Publishing:

Jeff Youngquist: VP Production & Special Projects
Caitlin O'Connell: Assistant Editor, Special Projects
Sven Larsen: Director, Licensed Publishing
David Gabriel: SVP Print, Sales & Marketing
C.B. Cebulski: Editor In Chief

IDW Publishing:

IDW

Collection Edits
JUSTIN EISINGER
and ALONZO SIMON

Collection Design
CHRISTA MIESNER

Cover Art by
ARIANNA FLOREAN

Chris Ryall, President and Publisher/CCO
Cara Morrison, Chief Financial Officer
Matt Ruzicka, Chief Accounting Officer
David Hedgecock, Associate Publisher
John Barber, Editor-In-Chief
Justin Eisinger, Editorial Director, Graphic Novels & Collections
Jerry Bennington, VP of New Product Development
Lorelei Bunjes, VP of Digital Services
Jud Meyers, Sales Director
Anna Morrow, Marketing Director
Tara McCrillis, Director of Design & Production
Mike Ford, Director of Operations
Rebekah Cahalin, General Manager

Ted Adams and Robbie Robbins, Founders of IDW

ISBN: 978-1-68405-523-4 23 22 21 20 1 2 3 4

Special thanks: Wil Moss

Originally published as MARVEL ACTION: BLACK PANTHER issues #4–6.

For international rights, contact licensing@idwpublishing.com

MARVEL

MARVEL ACTION

BLACK PANTHER

RISE TOGETHER

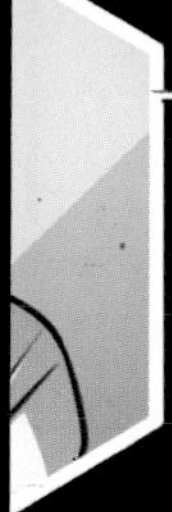

WRITTEN BY VITA AYALA

ART BY ARIANNA FLOREAN

ART ASSIST BY MARIO DEL PENNINO

COLORS BY MATTIA IACONO

COLOR ASSIST BY SARA MARTINELLI

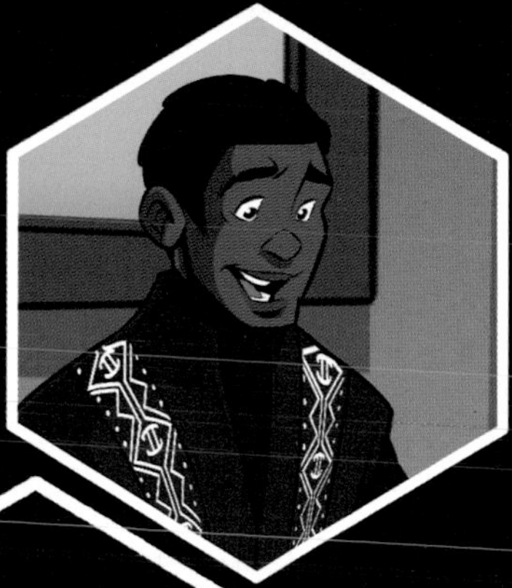

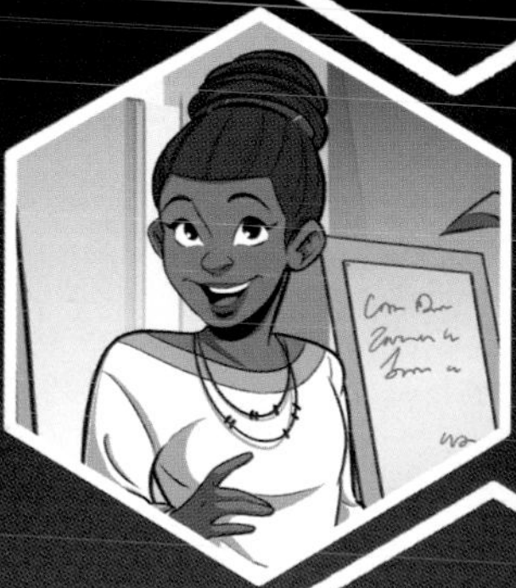

LETTERS BY TOM B. LONG & SHAWN LEE

ASSISTANT EDITOR ANNI PERHEENTUPA

ASSOCIATE EDITORS ELIZABETH BREI & CHASE MAROTZ

EDITOR DENTON J. TIPTON

EDITOR-IN-CHIEF JOHN BARBER

BLACK PANTHER CREATED BY STAN LEE & JACK KIRBY

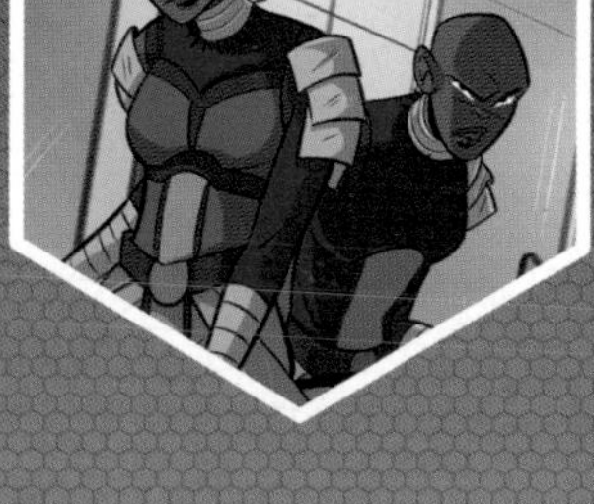

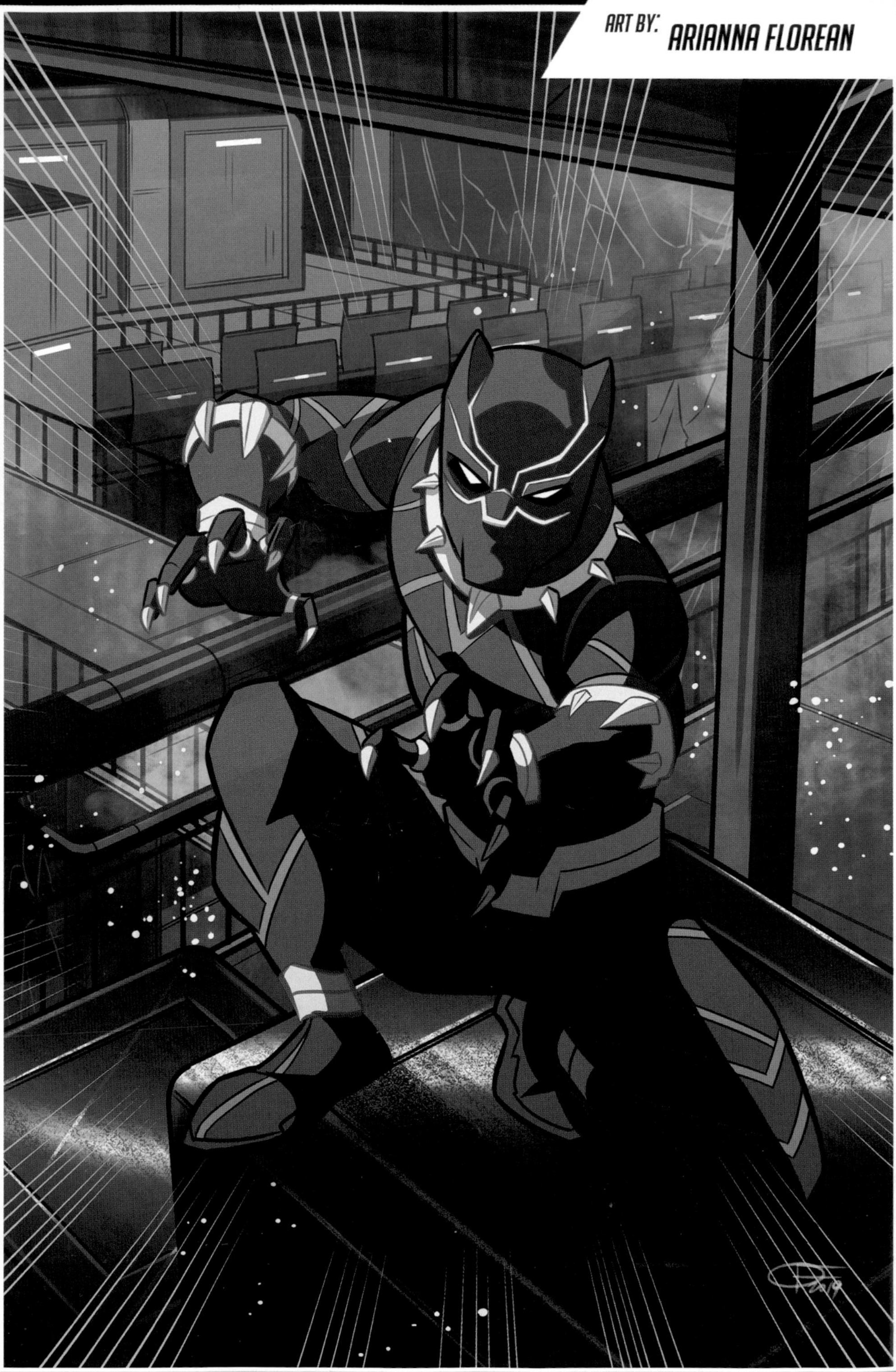
ART BY: ARIANNA FLOREAN

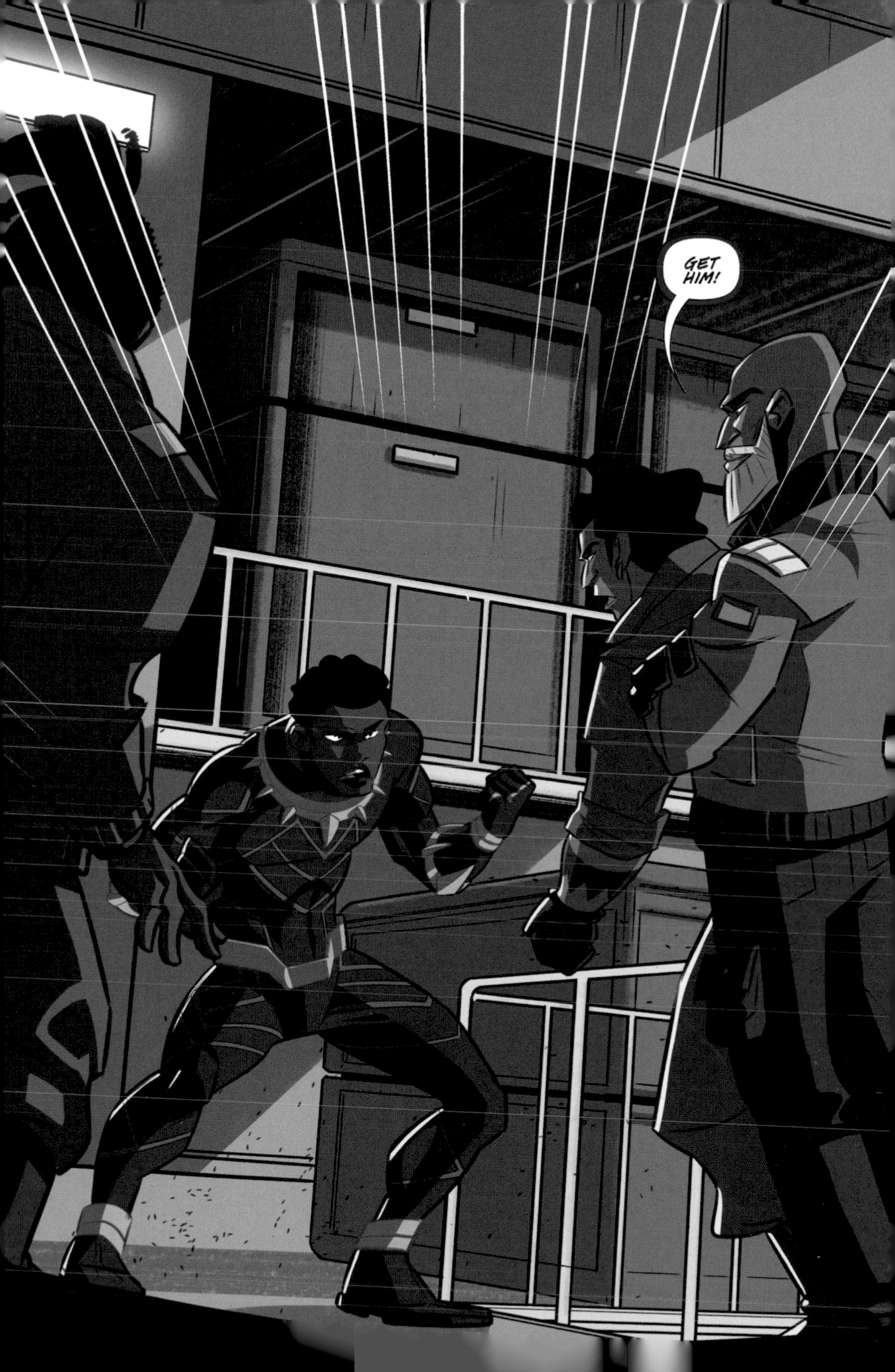
GET HIM!

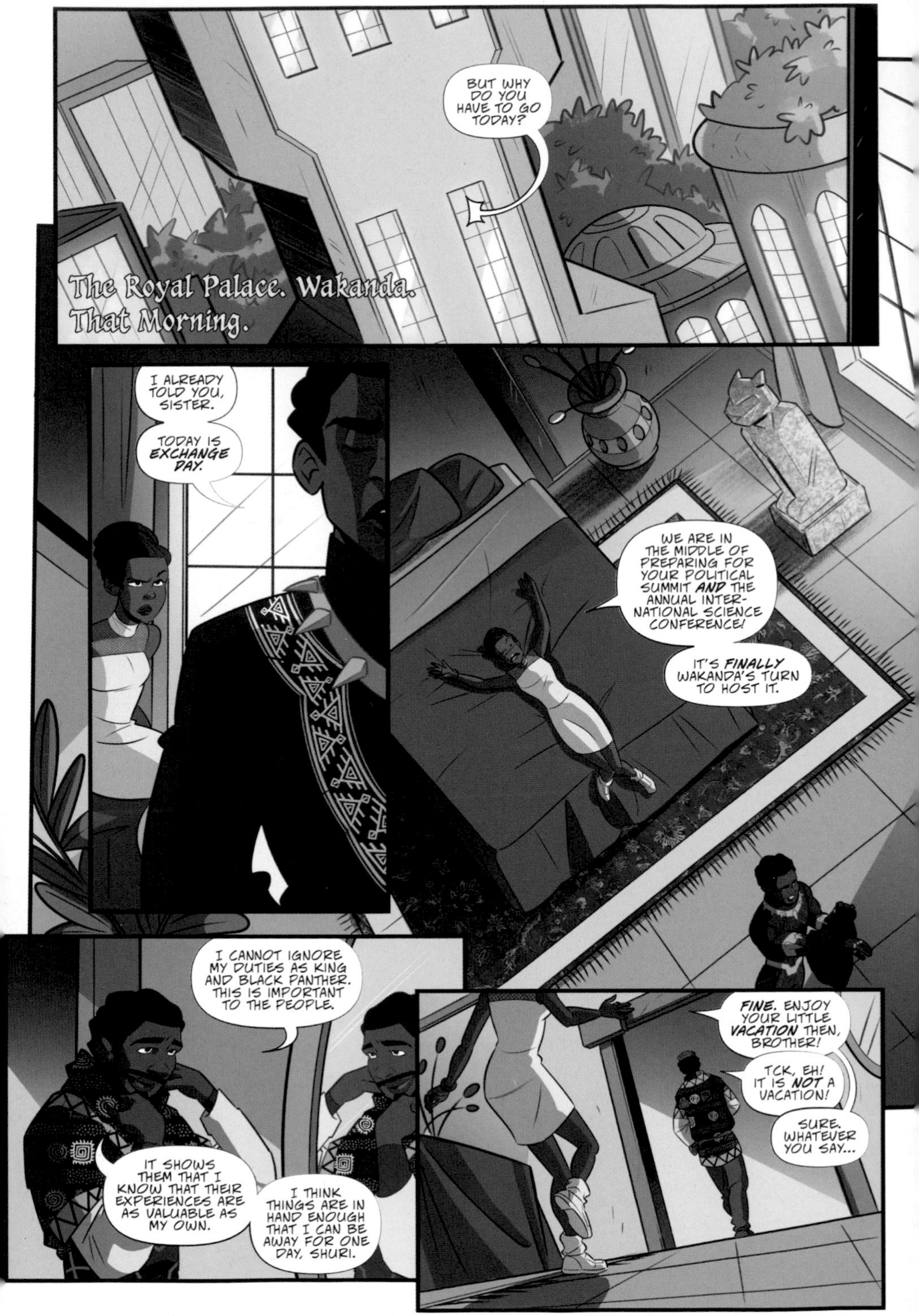
The Royal Palace. Wakanda. That Morning.
BUT WHY DO YOU HAVE TO GO TODAY?
I ALREADY TOLD YOU, SISTER.
TODAY IS EXCHANGE DAY.
WE ARE IN THE MIDDLE OF PREPARING FOR YOUR POLITICAL SUMMIT AND THE ANNUAL INTER-NATIONAL SCIENCE CONFERENCE!
IT'S FINALLY WAKANDA'S TURN TO HOST IT.
I CANNOT IGNORE MY DUTIES AS KING AND BLACK PANTHER. THIS IS IMPORTANT TO THE PEOPLE.
IT SHOWS THEM THAT I KNOW THAT THEIR EXPERIENCES ARE AS VALUABLE AS MY OWN.
I THINK THINGS ARE IN HAND ENOUGH THAT I CAN BE AWAY FOR ONE DAY, SHURI.
FINE. ENJOY YOUR LITTLE VACATION THEN, BROTHER!
TCK, EH! IT IS NOT A VACATION!
SURE. WHATEVER YOU SAY...

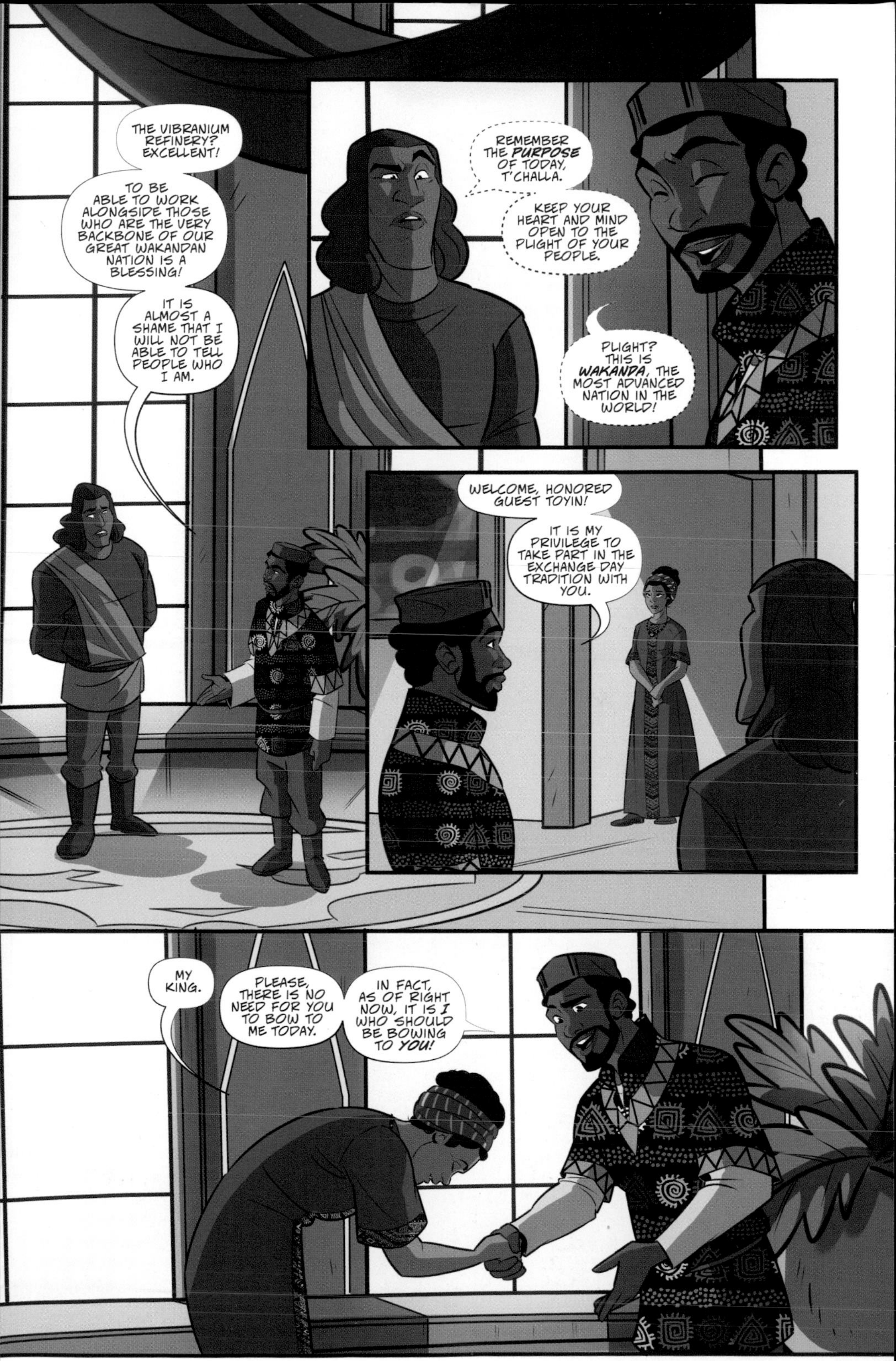
THE VIBRANIUM REFINERY? EXCELLENT!
TO BE ABLE TO WORK ALONGSIDE THOSE WHO ARE THE VERY BACKBONE OF OUR GREAT WAKANDAN NATION IS A BLESSING!
IT IS ALMOST A SHAME THAT I WILL NOT BE ABLE TO TELL PEOPLE WHO I AM.
REMEMBER THE PURPOSE OF TODAY, T'CHALLA.
KEEP YOUR HEART AND MIND OPEN TO THE PLIGHT OF YOUR PEOPLE.
PLIGHT? THIS IS WAKANDA, THE MOST ADVANCED NATION IN THE WORLD!
WELCOME, HONORED GUEST TOYIN!
IT IS MY PRIVILEGE TO TAKE PART IN THE EXCHANGE DAY TRADITION WITH YOU.
MY KING.
PLEASE, THERE IS NO NEED FOR YOU TO BOW TO ME TODAY.
IN FACT, AS OF RIGHT NOW, IT IS I WHO SHOULD BE BOWING TO YOU!

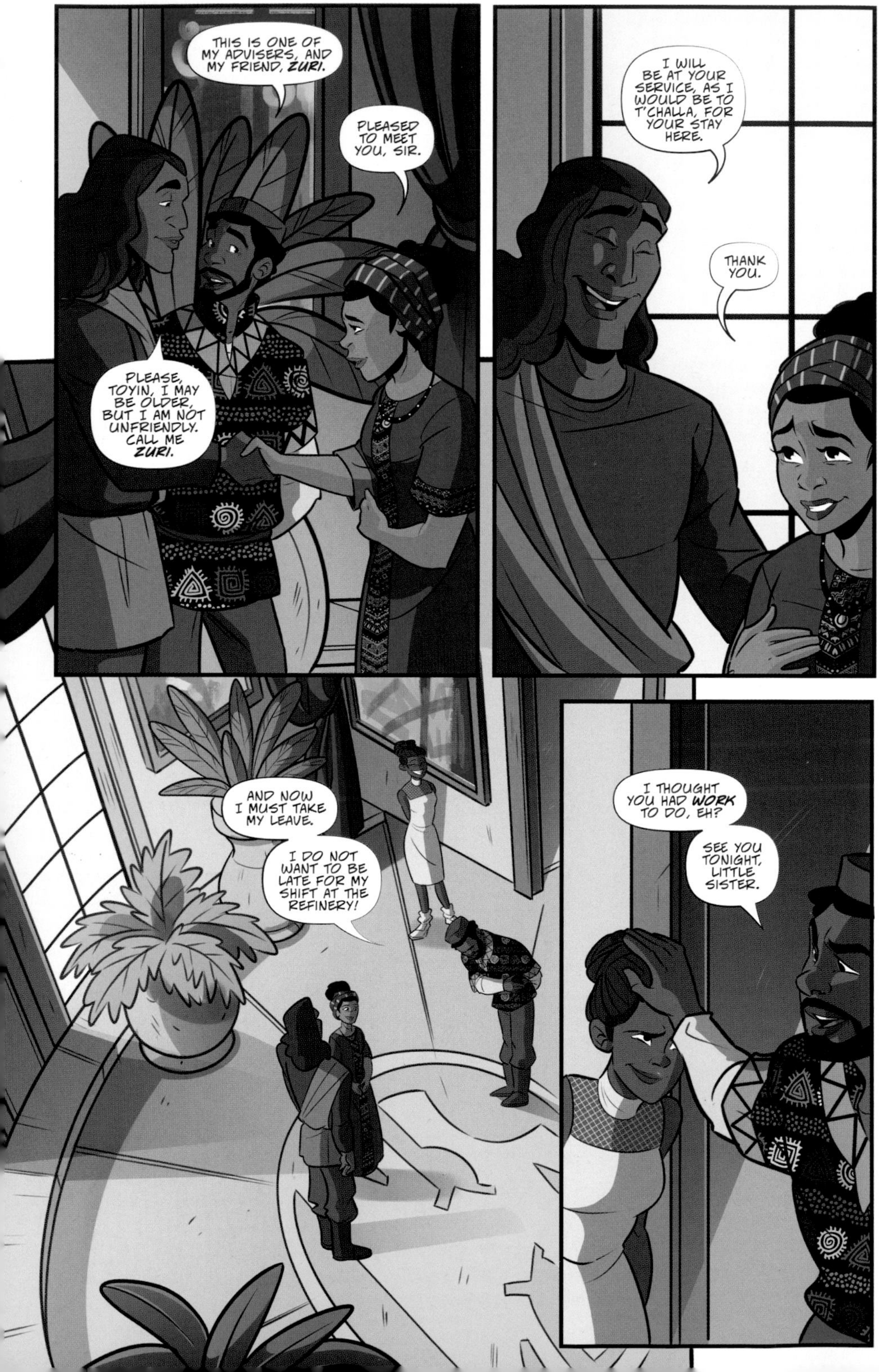
THIS IS ONE OF MY ADVISERS, AND MY FRIEND, ZURI.
PLEASED TO MEET YOU, SIR.
PLEASE, TOYIN, I MAY BE OLDER, BUT I AM NOT UNFRIENDLY. CALL ME ZURI.
I WILL BE AT YOUR SERVICE, AS I WOULD BE TO T'CHALLA, FOR YOUR STAY HERE.
THANK YOU.
AND NOW I MUST TAKE MY LEAVE.
I DO NOT WANT TO BE LATE FOR MY SHIFT AT THE REFINERY!
I THOUGHT YOU HAD WORK TO DO, EH?
SEE YOU TONIGHT, LITTLE SISTER.

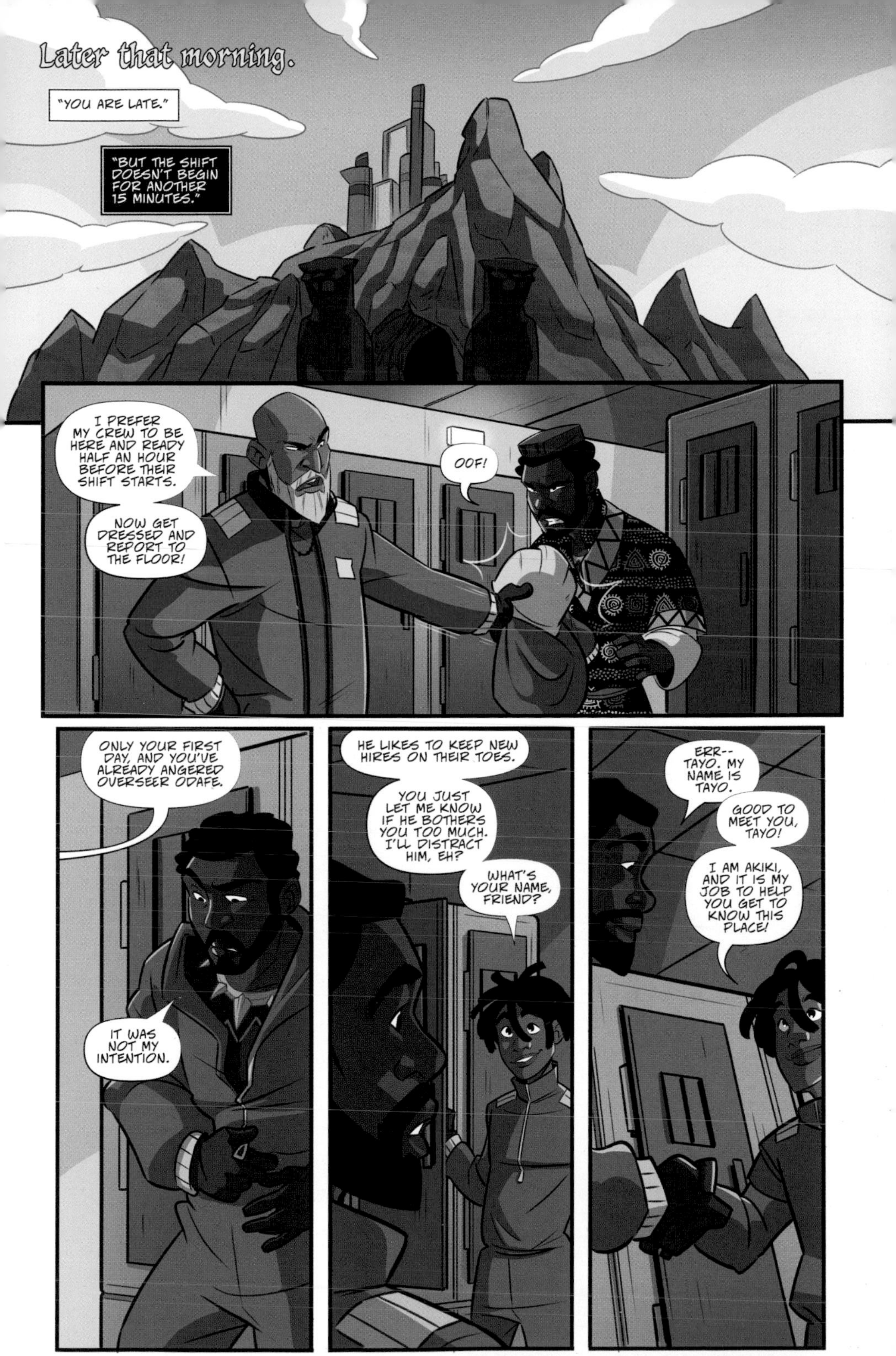
Later that morning.
"YOU ARE LATE."
"BUT THE SHIFT DOESN'T BEGIN FOR ANOTHER 15 MINUTES."
I PREFER MY CREW TO BE HERE AND READY HALF AN HOUR BEFORE THEIR SHIFT STARTS.
NOW GET DRESSED AND REPORT TO THE FLOOR!
OOF!
ONLY YOUR FIRST DAY, AND YOU'VE ALREADY ANGERED OVERSEER ODAFE.
IT WAS NOT MY INTENTION.
HE LIKES TO KEEP NEW HIRES ON THEIR TOES.
YOU JUST LET ME KNOW IF HE BOTHERS YOU TOO MUCH. I'LL DISTRACT HIM, EH?
WHAT'S YOUR NAME, FRIEND?
ERR-- TAYO. MY NAME IS TAYO.
GOOD TO MEET YOU, TAYO!
I AM AKIKI, AND IT IS MY JOB TO HELP YOU GET TO KNOW THIS PLACE!

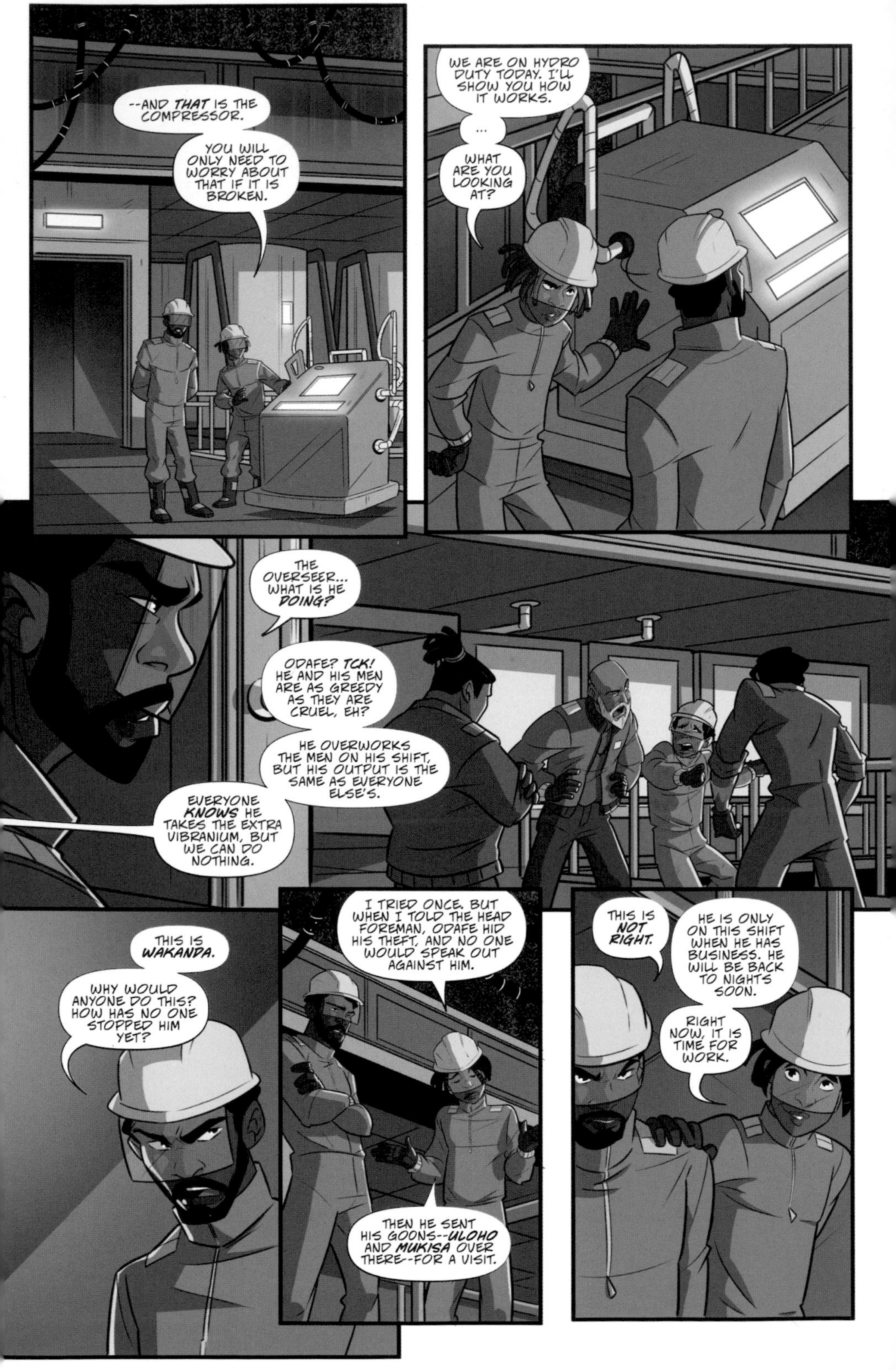
--AND *THAT* IS THE COMPRESSOR.
YOU WILL ONLY NEED TO WORRY ABOUT THAT IF IT IS BROKEN.
WE ARE ON HYDRO DUTY TODAY. I'LL SHOW YOU HOW IT WORKS.
...
WHAT ARE YOU LOOKING AT?
THE OVERSEER... WHAT IS HE *DOING?*
ODAFE? *TCK!* HE AND HIS MEN ARE AS GREEDY AS THEY ARE CRUEL, EH?
HE OVERWORKS THE MEN ON HIS SHIFT, BUT HIS OUTPUT IS THE SAME AS EVERYONE ELSE'S.
EVERYONE *KNOWS* HE TAKES THE EXTRA VIBRANIUM, BUT WE CAN DO NOTHING.
THIS IS *WAKANDA.*
WHY WOULD ANYONE DO THIS? HOW HAS NO ONE STOPPED HIM YET?
I TRIED ONCE. BUT WHEN I TOLD THE HEAD FOREMAN, ODAFE HID HIS THEFT, AND NO ONE WOULD SPEAK OUT AGAINST HIM.
THEN HE SENT HIS GOONS--*ULOHO* AND *MUKISA* OVER THERE--FOR A VISIT.
THIS IS *NOT RIGHT.*
HE IS ONLY ON THIS SHIFT WHEN HE HAS BUSINESS. HE WILL BE BACK TO NIGHTS SOON.
RIGHT NOW, IT IS TIME FOR WORK.

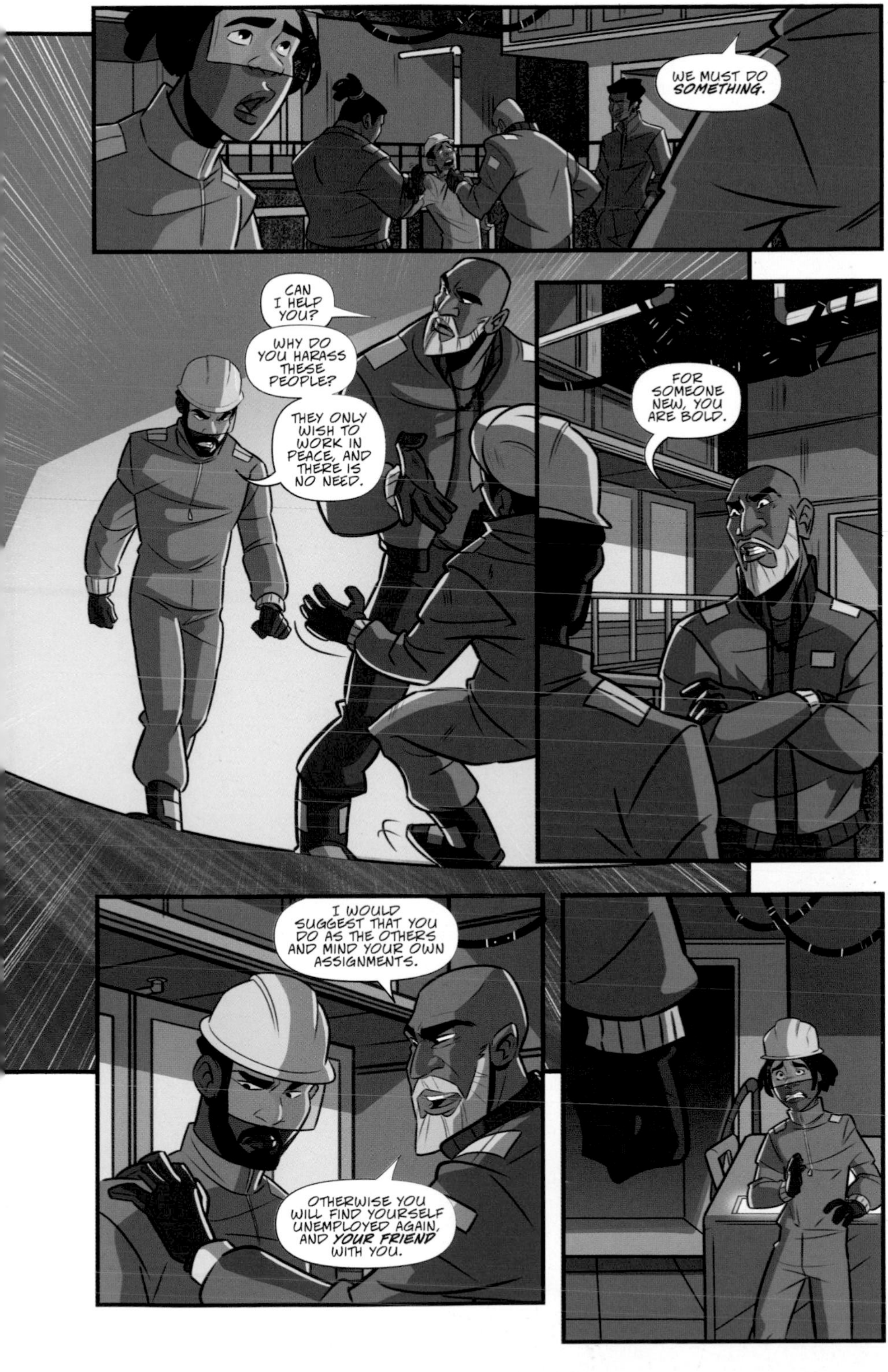
WE MUST DO *SOMETHING.*
CAN I HELP YOU?
WHY DO YOU HARASS THESE PEOPLE?
THEY ONLY WISH TO WORK IN PEACE, AND THERE IS NO NEED.
FOR SOMEONE NEW, YOU ARE BOLD.
I WOULD SUGGEST THAT YOU DO AS THE OTHERS AND MIND YOUR OWN ASSIGNMENTS.
OTHERWISE YOU WILL FIND YOURSELF UNEMPLOYED AGAIN, AND *YOUR FRIEND* WITH YOU.

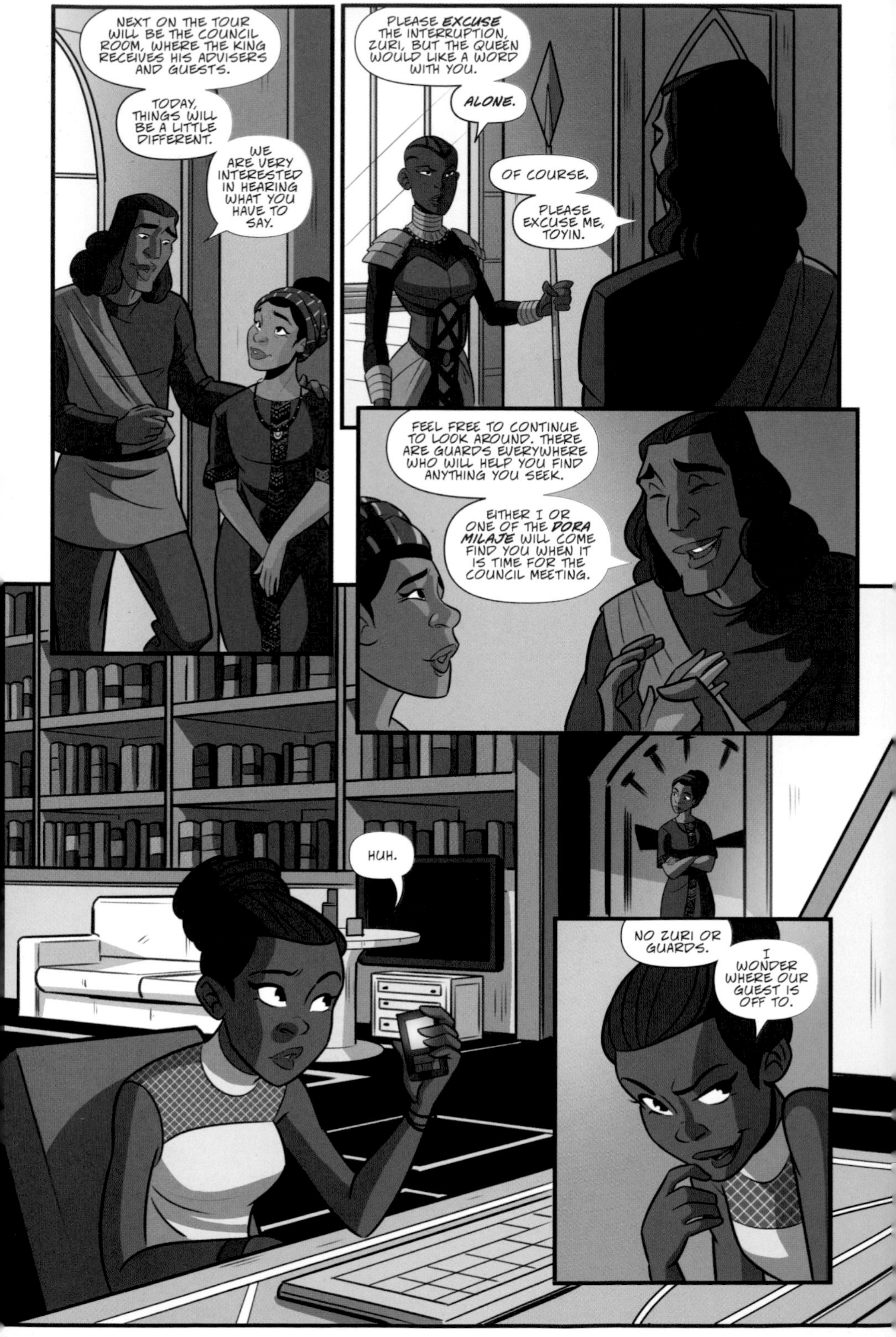
NEXT ON THE TOUR WILL BE THE COUNCIL ROOM, WHERE THE KING RECEIVES HIS ADVISERS AND GUESTS.
TODAY, THINGS WILL BE A LITTLE DIFFERENT.
WE ARE VERY INTERESTED IN HEARING WHAT YOU HAVE TO SAY.
PLEASE EXCUSE THE INTERRUPTION, ZURI, BUT THE QUEEN WOULD LIKE A WORD WITH YOU.
ALONE.
OF COURSE.
PLEASE EXCUSE ME, TOYIN.
FEEL FREE TO CONTINUE TO LOOK AROUND. THERE ARE GUARDS EVERYWHERE WHO WILL HELP YOU FIND ANYTHING YOU SEEK.
EITHER I OR ONE OF THE DORA MILAJE WILL COME FIND YOU WHEN IT IS TIME FOR THE COUNCIL MEETING.
HUH.
NO ZURI OR GUARDS.
I WONDER WHERE OUR GUEST IS OFF TO.

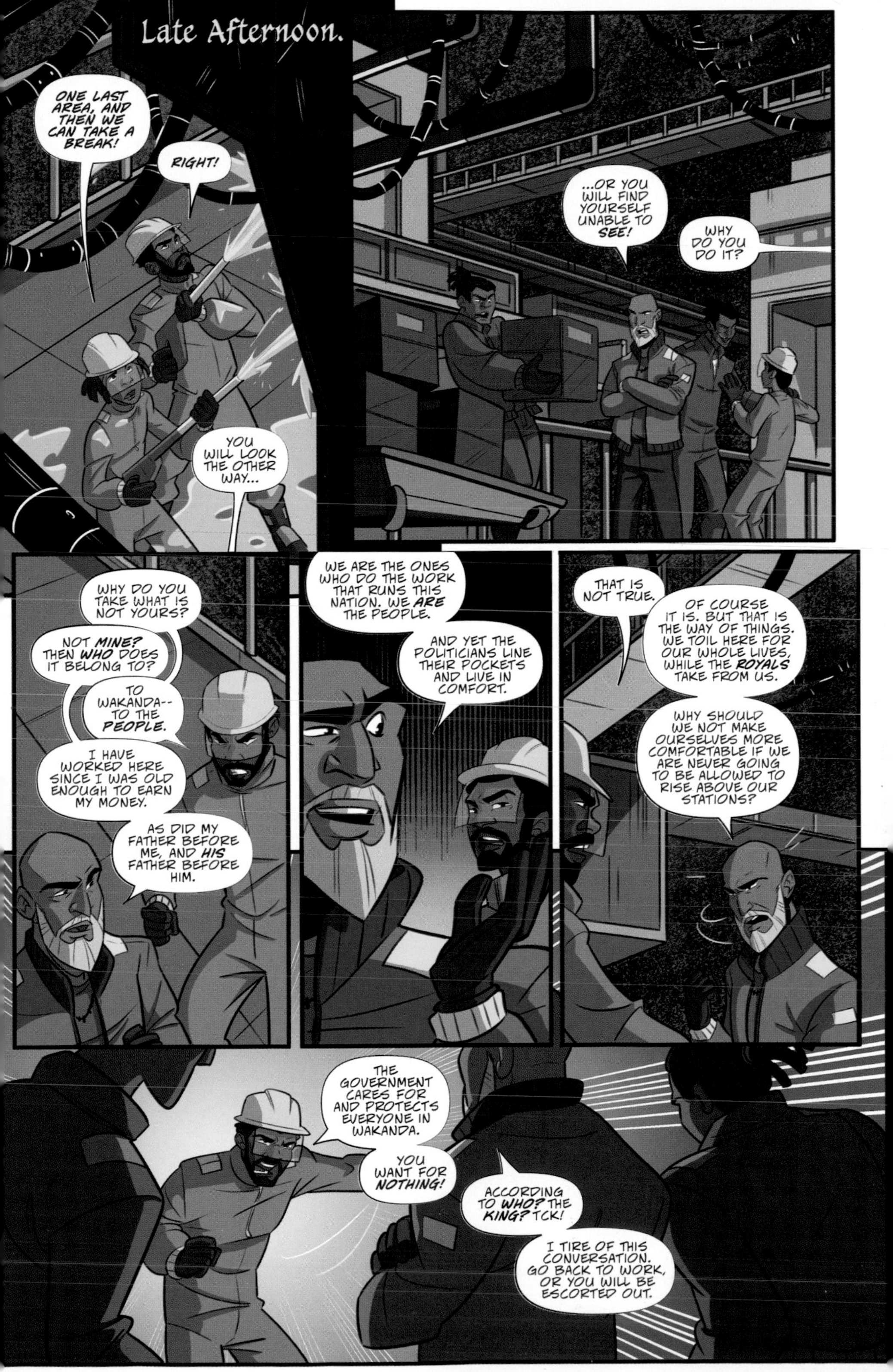

Late Afternoon.
ONE LAST AREA, AND THEN WE CAN TAKE A BREAK!
RIGHT!
YOU WILL LOOK THE OTHER WAY...
...OR YOU WILL FIND YOURSELF UNABLE TO SEE!
WHY DO YOU DO IT?
WHY DO YOU TAKE WHAT IS NOT YOURS?
NOT MINE? THEN WHO DOES IT BELONG TO?
TO WAKANDA-- TO THE PEOPLE.
I HAVE WORKED HERE SINCE I WAS OLD ENOUGH TO EARN MY MONEY.
AS DID MY FATHER BEFORE ME, AND HIS FATHER BEFORE HIM.
WE ARE THE ONES WHO DO THE WORK THAT RUNS THIS NATION. WE ARE THE PEOPLE.
AND YET THE POLITICIANS LINE THEIR POCKETS AND LIVE IN COMFORT.
THAT IS NOT TRUE.
OF COURSE IT IS. BUT THAT IS THE WAY OF THINGS. WE TOIL HERE FOR OUR WHOLE LIVES, WHILE THE ROYALS TAKE FROM US.
WHY SHOULD WE NOT MAKE OURSELVES MORE COMFORTABLE IF WE ARE NEVER GOING TO BE ALLOWED TO RISE ABOVE OUR STATIONS?
THE GOVERNMENT CARES FOR AND PROTECTS EVERYONE IN WAKANDA.
YOU WANT FOR NOTHING!
ACCORDING TO WHO? THE KING? TCK!
I TIRE OF THIS CONVERSATION. GO BACK TO WORK, OR YOU WILL BE ESCORTED OUT.

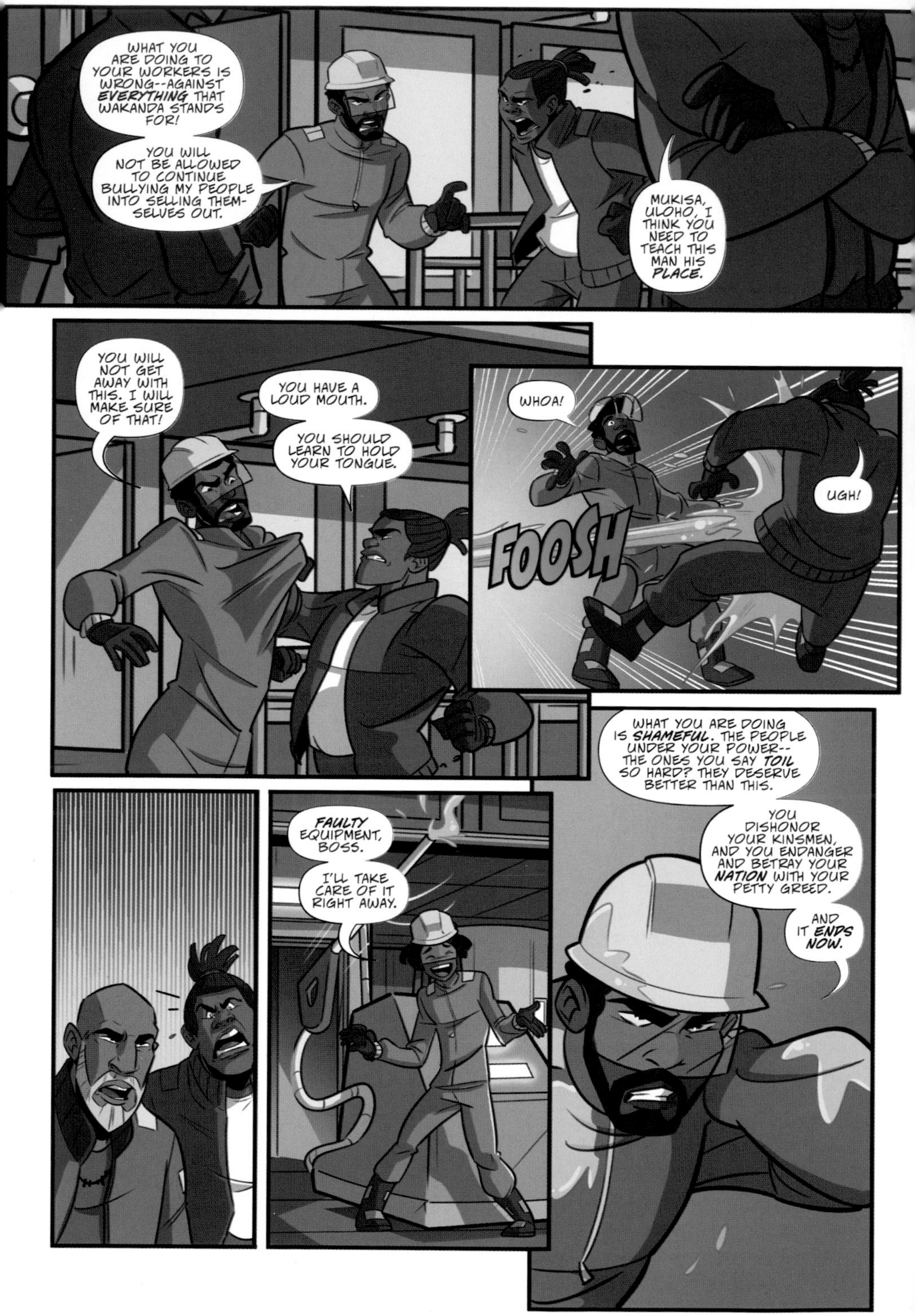
WHAT YOU ARE DOING TO YOUR WORKERS IS WRONG--AGAINST EVERYTHING THAT WAKANDA STANDS FOR!
YOU WILL NOT BE ALLOWED TO CONTINUE BULLYING MY PEOPLE INTO SELLING THEMSELVES OUT.
MUKISA, ULOHO, I THINK YOU NEED TO TEACH THIS MAN HIS PLACE.
YOU WILL NOT GET AWAY WITH THIS. I WILL MAKE SURE OF THAT!
YOU HAVE A LOUD MOUTH.
YOU SHOULD LEARN TO HOLD YOUR TONGUE.
WHOA!
UGH!
FOOSH
WHAT YOU ARE DOING IS SHAMEFUL. THE PEOPLE UNDER YOUR POWER-- THE ONES YOU SAY TOIL SO HARD? THEY DESERVE BETTER THAN THIS.
FAULTY EQUIPMENT, BOSS.
I'LL TAKE CARE OF IT RIGHT AWAY.
YOU DISHONOR YOUR KINSMEN, AND YOU ENDANGER AND BETRAY YOUR NATION WITH YOUR PETTY GREED.
AND IT ENDS NOW.

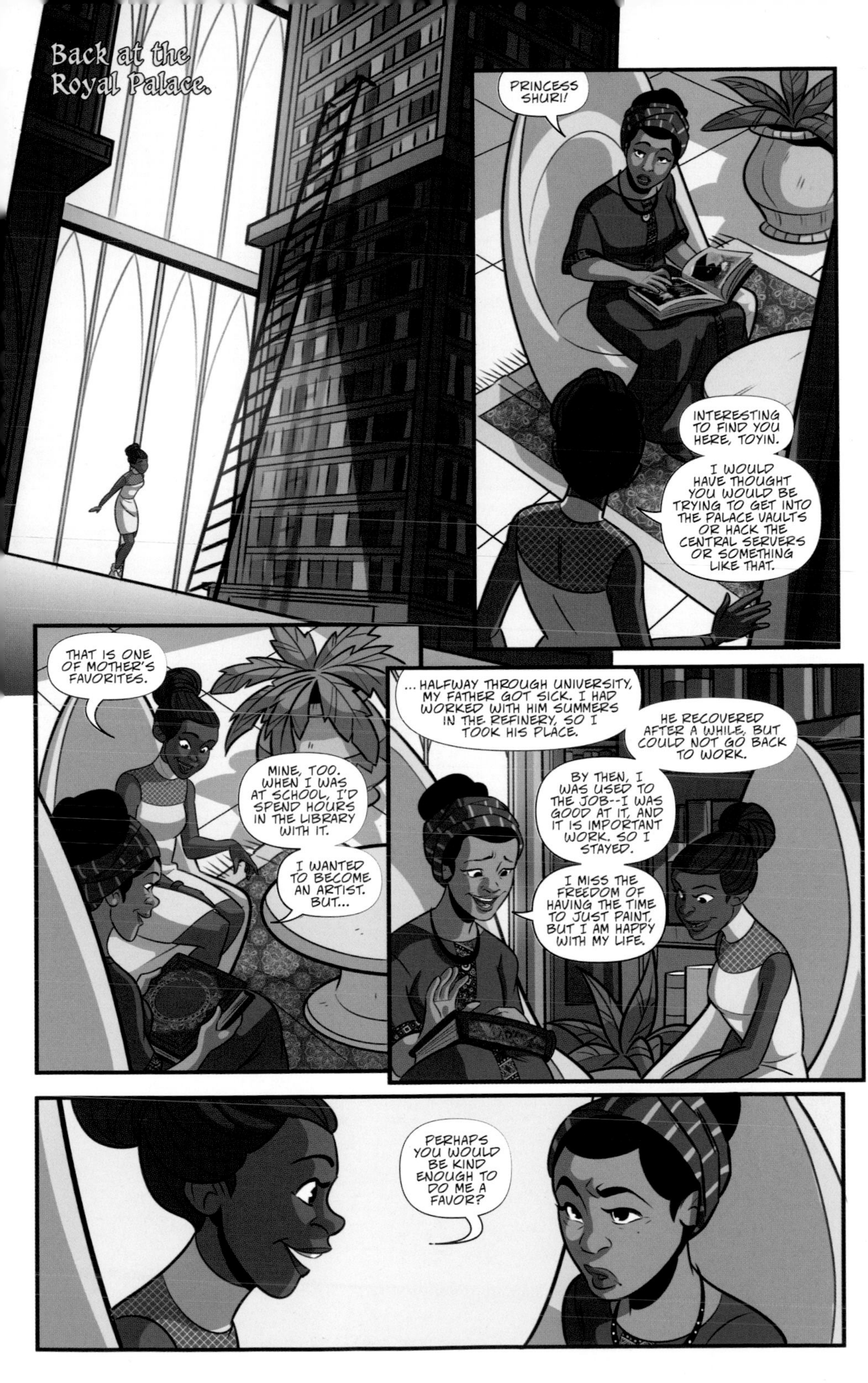
Back at the Royal Palace.
PRINCESS SHURI!
INTERESTING TO FIND YOU HERE, TOYIN.
I WOULD HAVE THOUGHT YOU WOULD BE TRYING TO GET INTO THE PALACE VAULTS OR HACK THE CENTRAL SERVERS OR SOMETHING LIKE THAT.
THAT IS ONE OF MOTHER'S FAVORITES.
MINE, TOO. WHEN I WAS AT SCHOOL, I'D SPEND HOURS IN THE LIBRARY WITH IT.
I WANTED TO BECOME AN ARTIST. BUT...
...HALFWAY THROUGH UNIVERSITY, MY FATHER GOT SICK. I HAD WORKED WITH HIM SUMMERS IN THE REFINERY, SO I TOOK HIS PLACE.
HE RECOVERED AFTER A WHILE, BUT COULD NOT GO BACK TO WORK.
BY THEN, I WAS USED TO THE JOB--I WAS GOOD AT IT, AND IT IS IMPORTANT WORK. SO I STAYED.
I MISS THE FREEDOM OF HAVING THE TIME TO JUST PAINT, BUT I AM HAPPY WITH MY LIFE.
PERHAPS YOU WOULD BE KIND ENOUGH TO DO ME A FAVOR?

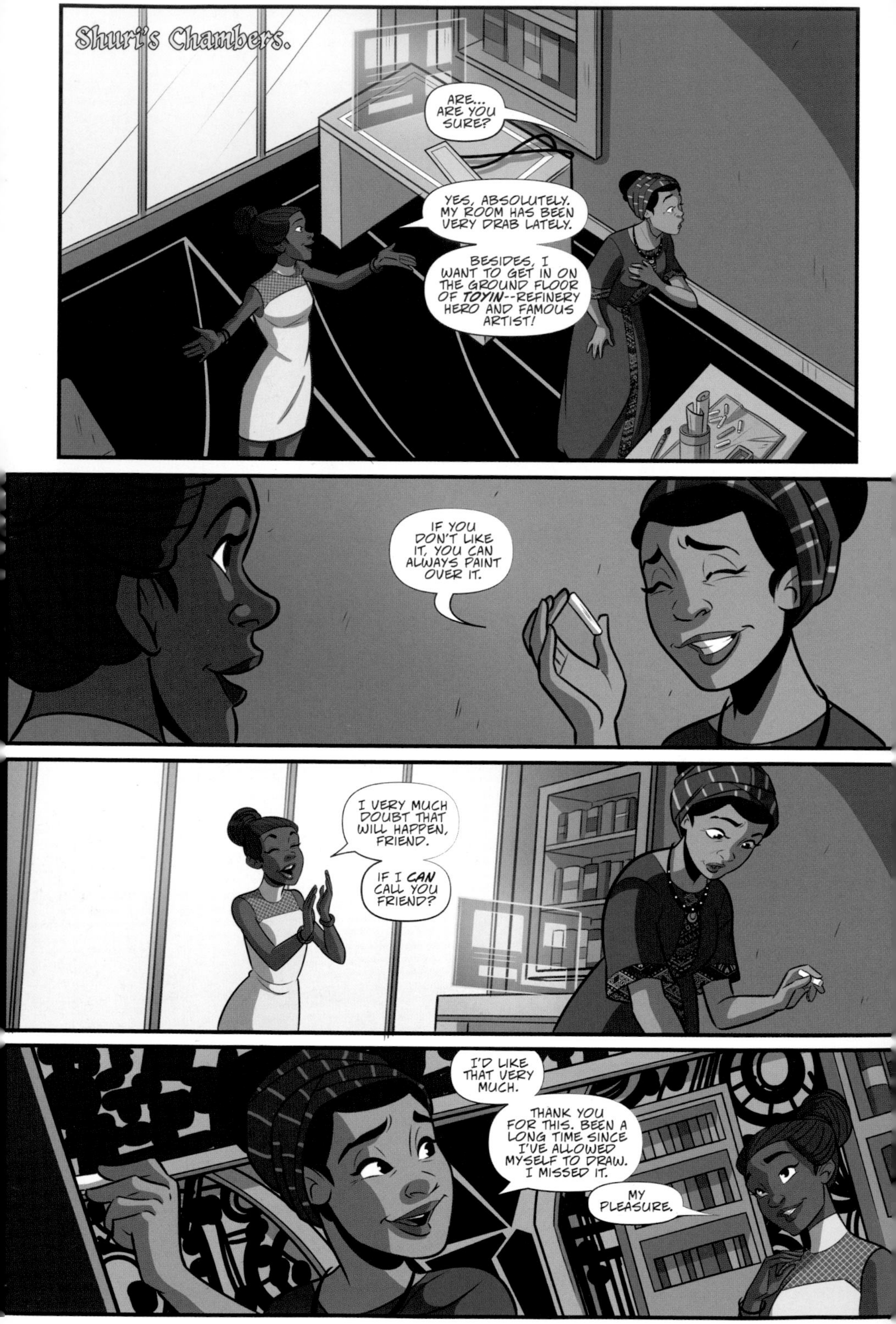
Shuri's Chambers.
ARE... ARE YOU SURE?
YES, ABSOLUTELY. MY ROOM HAS BEEN VERY DRAB LATELY.
BESIDES, I WANT TO GET IN ON THE GROUND FLOOR OF TOYIN--REFINERY HERO AND FAMOUS ARTIST!
IF YOU DON'T LIKE IT, YOU CAN ALWAYS PAINT OVER IT.
I VERY MUCH DOUBT THAT WILL HAPPEN, FRIEND.
IF I CAN CALL YOU FRIEND?
I'D LIKE THAT VERY MUCH.
THANK YOU FOR THIS. BEEN A LONG TIME SINCE I'VE ALLOWED MYSELF TO DRAW. I MISSED IT.
MY PLEASURE.

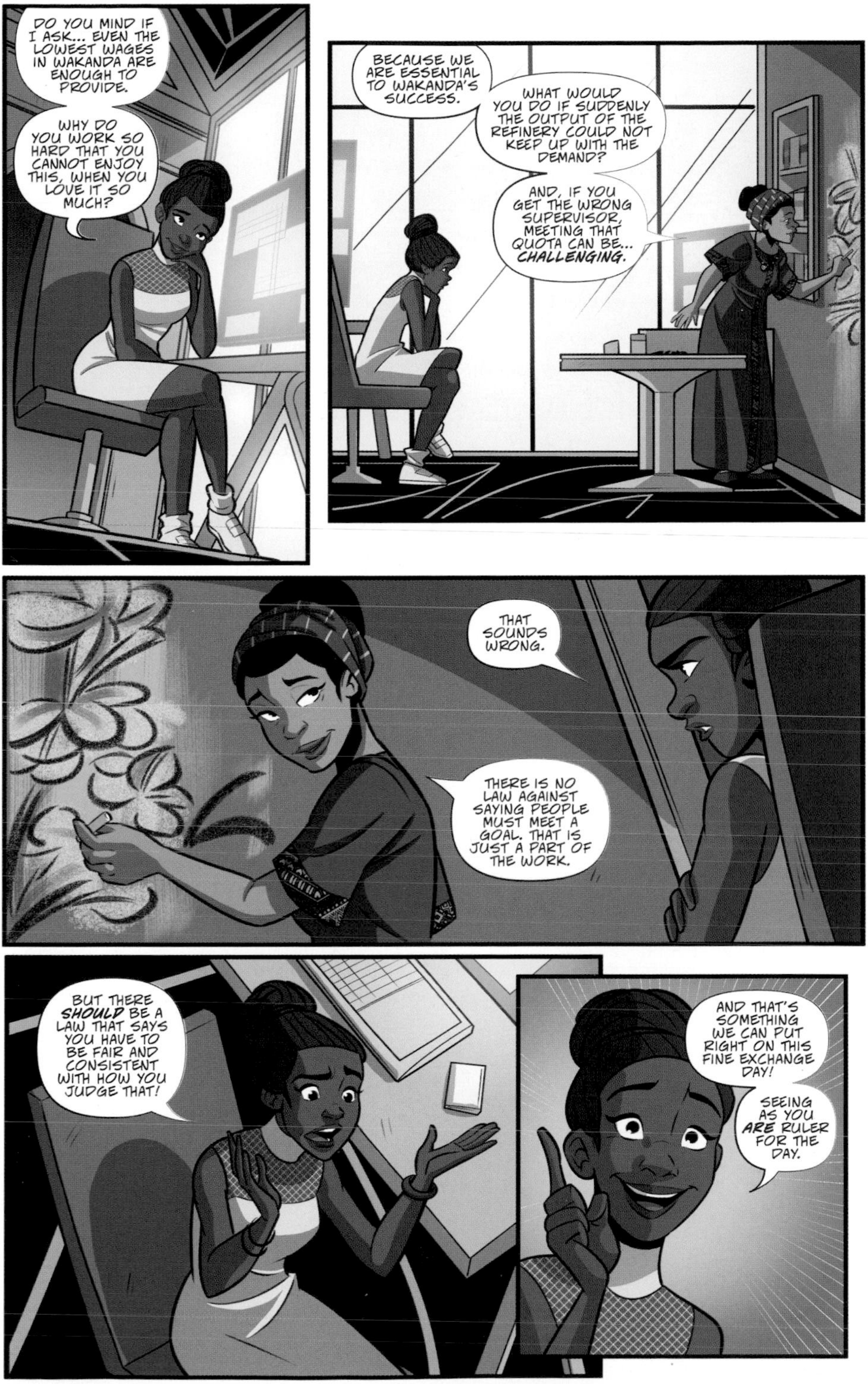

DO YOU MIND IF I ASK... EVEN THE LOWEST WAGES IN WAKANDA ARE ENOUGH TO PROVIDE.
WHY DO YOU WORK SO HARD THAT YOU CANNOT ENJOY THIS, WHEN YOU LOVE IT SO MUCH?
BECAUSE WE ARE ESSENTIAL TO WAKANDA'S SUCCESS.
WHAT WOULD YOU DO IF SUDDENLY THE OUTPUT OF THE REFINERY COULD NOT KEEP UP WITH THE DEMAND?
AND, IF YOU GET THE WRONG SUPERVISOR, MEETING THAT QUOTA CAN BE... CHALLENGING.
THAT SOUNDS WRONG.
THERE IS NO LAW AGAINST SAYING PEOPLE MUST MEET A GOAL. THAT IS JUST A PART OF THE WORK.
BUT THERE SHOULD BE A LAW THAT SAYS YOU HAVE TO BE FAIR AND CONSISTENT WITH HOW YOU JUDGE THAT!
AND THAT'S SOMETHING WE CAN PUT RIGHT ON THIS FINE EXCHANGE DAY!
SEEING AS YOU ARE RULER FOR THE DAY.

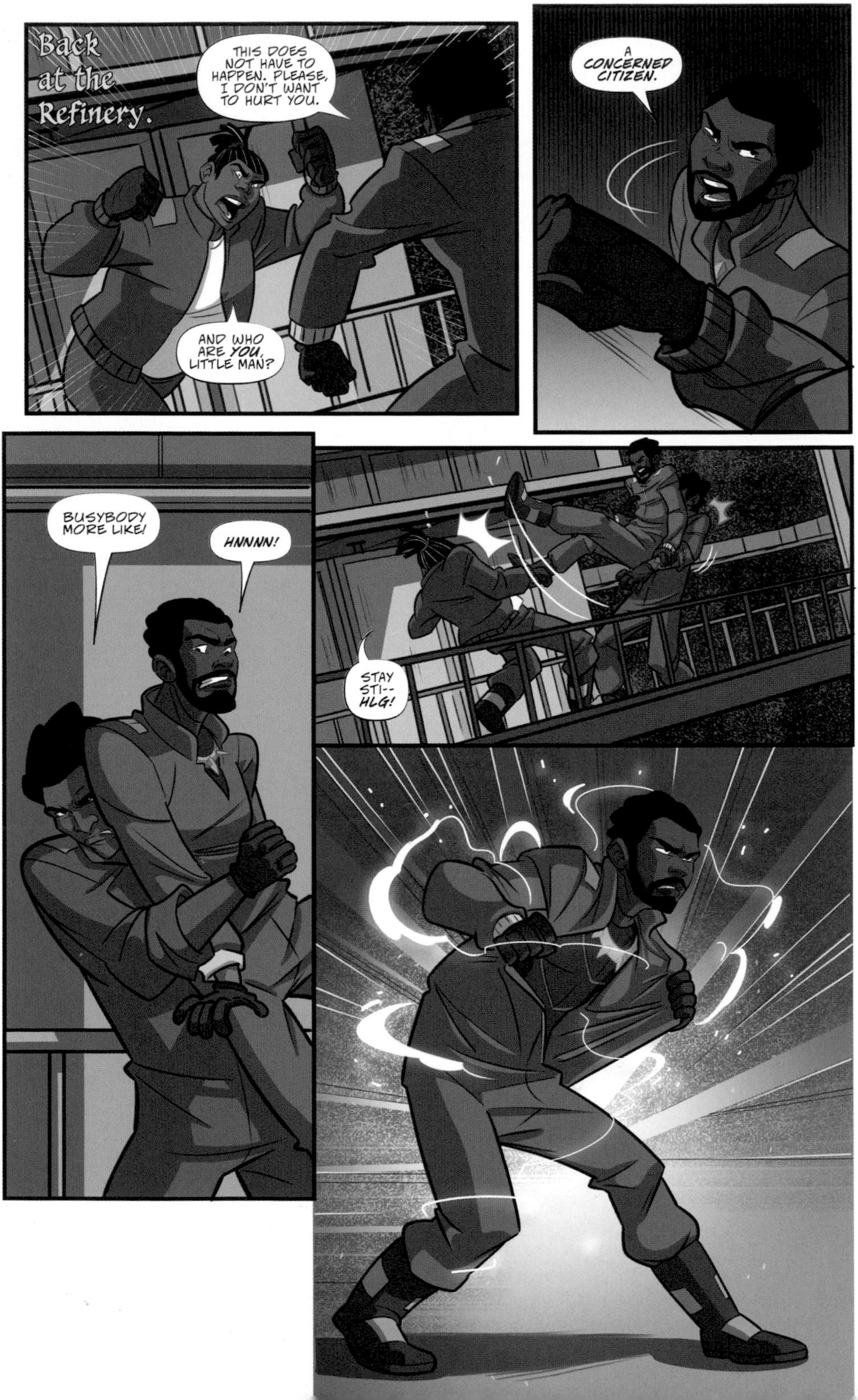
Back at the Refinery.
THIS DOES NOT HAVE TO HAPPEN. PLEASE, I DON'T WANT TO HURT YOU.
AND WHO ARE YOU, LITTLE MAN?
A CONCERNED CITIZEN.
BUSYBODY MORE LIKE!
HNNNN!
STAY STI-- HLG!

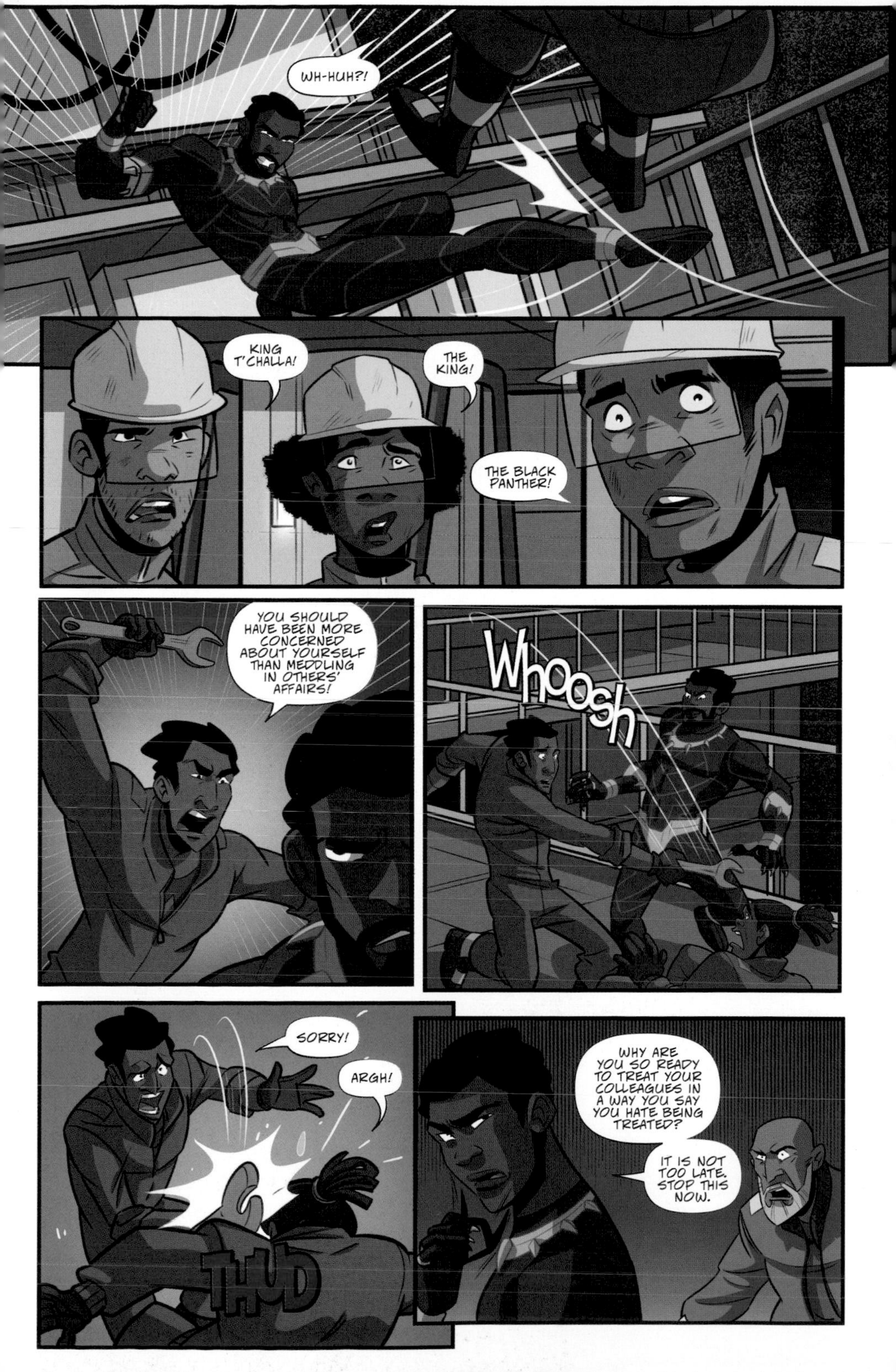
WH-HUH?!
KING T'CHALLA!
THE KING!
THE BLACK PANTHER!
YOU SHOULD HAVE BEEN MORE CONCERNED ABOUT YOURSELF THAN MEDDLING IN OTHERS' AFFAIRS!
Whoosh
SORRY!
ARGH!
THUD
WHY ARE YOU SO READY TO TREAT YOUR COLLEAGUES IN A WAY YOU SAY YOU HATE BEING TREATED?
IT IS NOT TOO LATE. STOP THIS NOW.

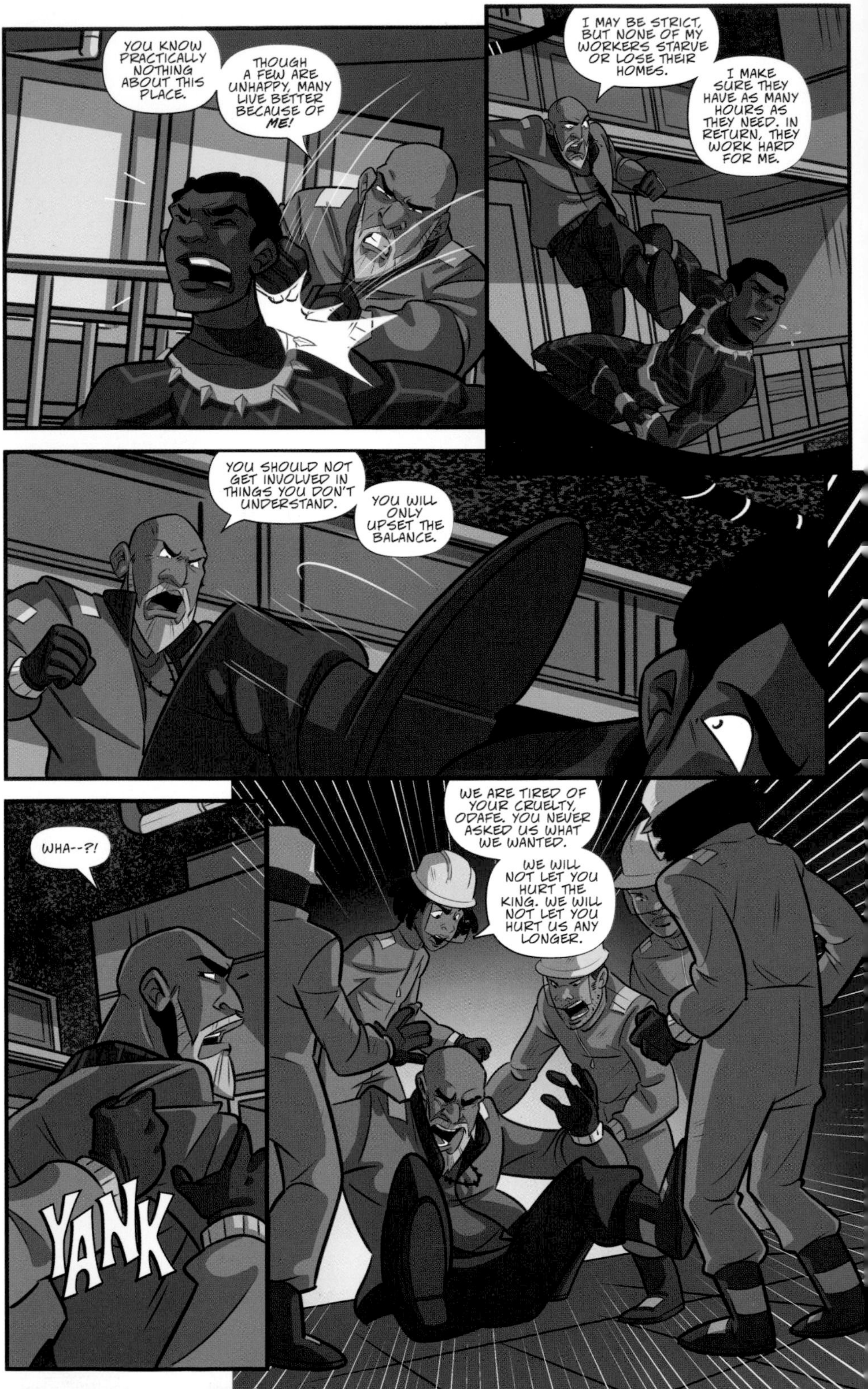
YOU KNOW PRACTICALLY NOTHING ABOUT THIS PLACE.
THOUGH A FEW ARE UNHAPPY, MANY LIVE BETTER BECAUSE OF *ME!*
I MAY BE STRICT, BUT NONE OF MY WORKERS STARVE OR LOSE THEIR HOMES.
I MAKE SURE THEY HAVE AS MANY HOURS AS THEY NEED. IN RETURN, THEY WORK HARD FOR ME.
YOU SHOULD NOT GET INVOLVED IN THINGS YOU DON'T UNDERSTAND.
YOU WILL ONLY UPSET THE BALANCE.
WHA--?!
YANK
WE ARE TIRED OF YOUR CRUELTY, ODAFE. YOU NEVER ASKED US WHAT WE WANTED.
WE WILL NOT LET YOU HURT THE KING. WE WILL NOT LET YOU HURT US ANY LONGER.

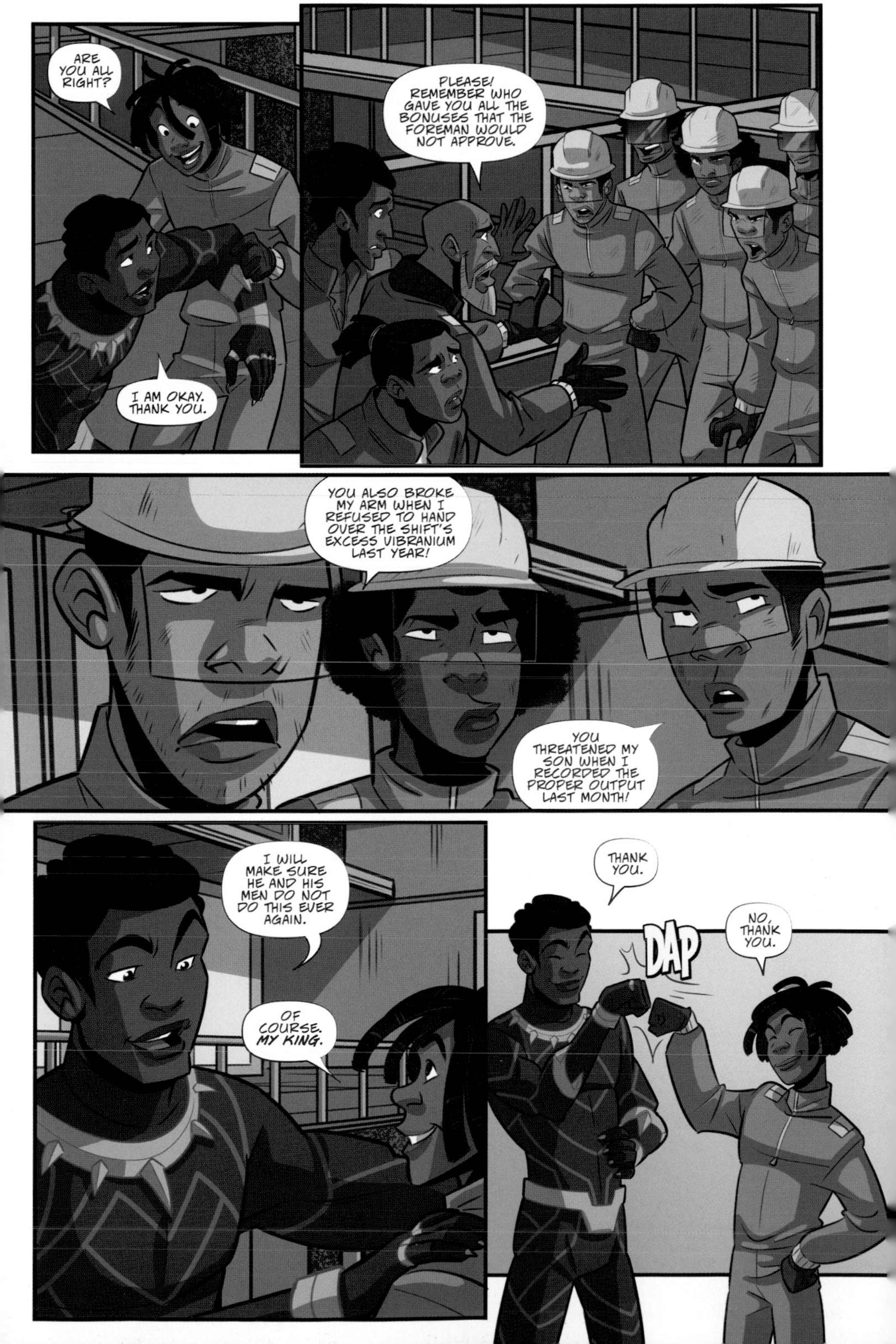
ARE YOU ALL RIGHT?
I AM OKAY. THANK YOU.
PLEASE! REMEMBER WHO GAVE YOU ALL THE BONUSES THAT THE FOREMAN WOULD NOT APPROVE.
YOU ALSO BROKE MY ARM WHEN I REFUSED TO HAND OVER THE SHIFT'S EXCESS VIBRANIUM LAST YEAR!
YOU THREATENED MY SON WHEN I RECORDED THE PROPER OUTPUT LAST MONTH!
I WILL MAKE SURE HE AND HIS MEN DO NOT DO THIS EVER AGAIN.
OF COURSE. *MY KING.*
THANK YOU.
DAP
NO, THANK YOU.

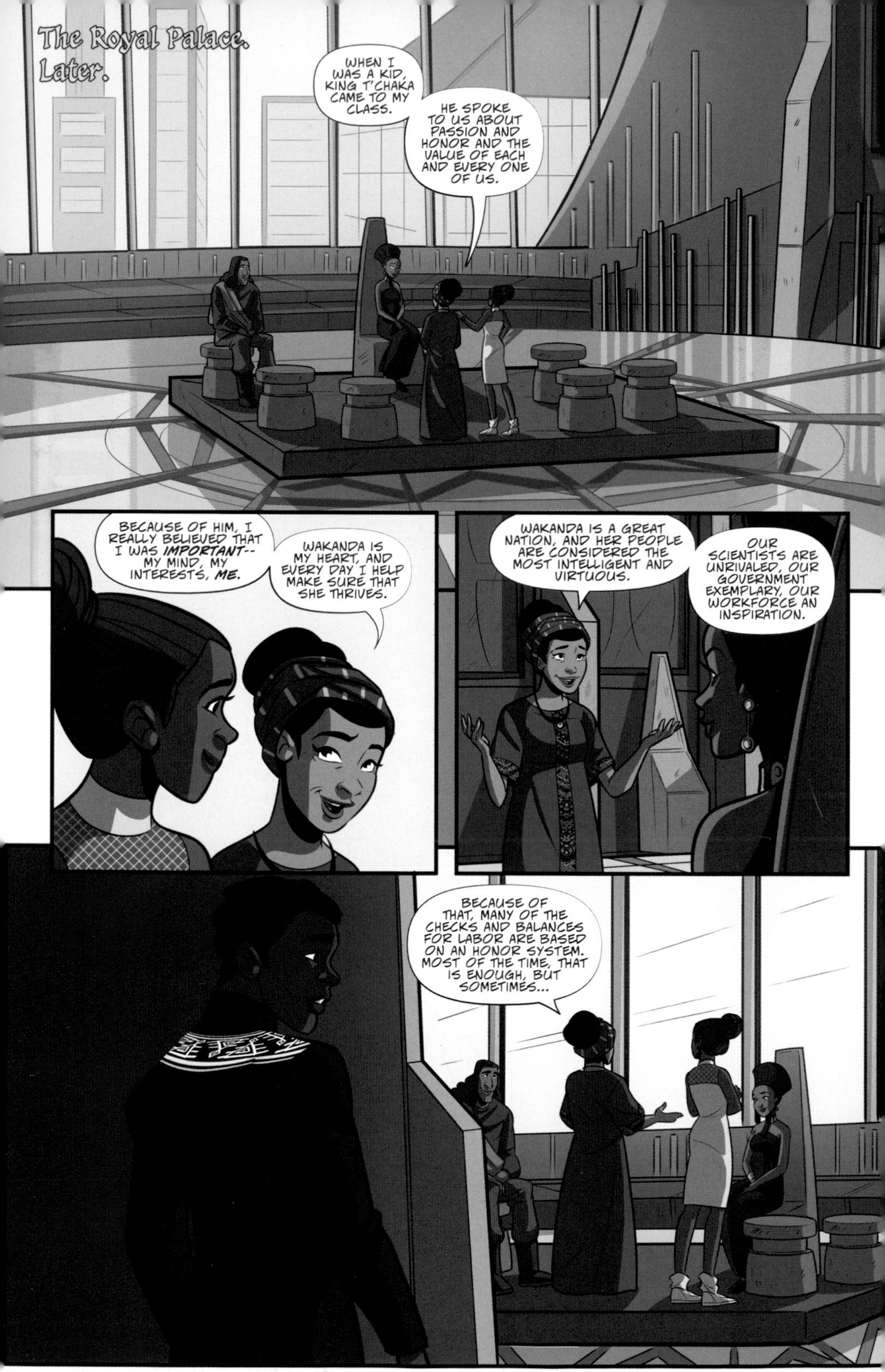
The Royal Palace. Later.
WHEN I WAS A KID, KING T'CHAKA CAME TO MY CLASS.
HE SPOKE TO US ABOUT PASSION AND HONOR AND THE VALUE OF EACH AND EVERY ONE OF US.
BECAUSE OF HIM, I REALLY BELIEVED THAT I WAS IMPORTANT-- MY MIND, MY INTERESTS, ME.
WAKANDA IS MY HEART, AND EVERY DAY I HELP MAKE SURE THAT SHE THRIVES.
WAKANDA IS A GREAT NATION, AND HER PEOPLE ARE CONSIDERED THE MOST INTELLIGENT AND VIRTUOUS.
OUR SCIENTISTS ARE UNRIVALED, OUR GOVERNMENT EXEMPLARY, OUR WORKFORCE AN INSPIRATION.
BECAUSE OF THAT, MANY OF THE CHECKS AND BALANCES FOR LABOR ARE BASED ON AN HONOR SYSTEM. MOST OF THE TIME, THAT IS ENOUGH, BUT SOMETIMES...

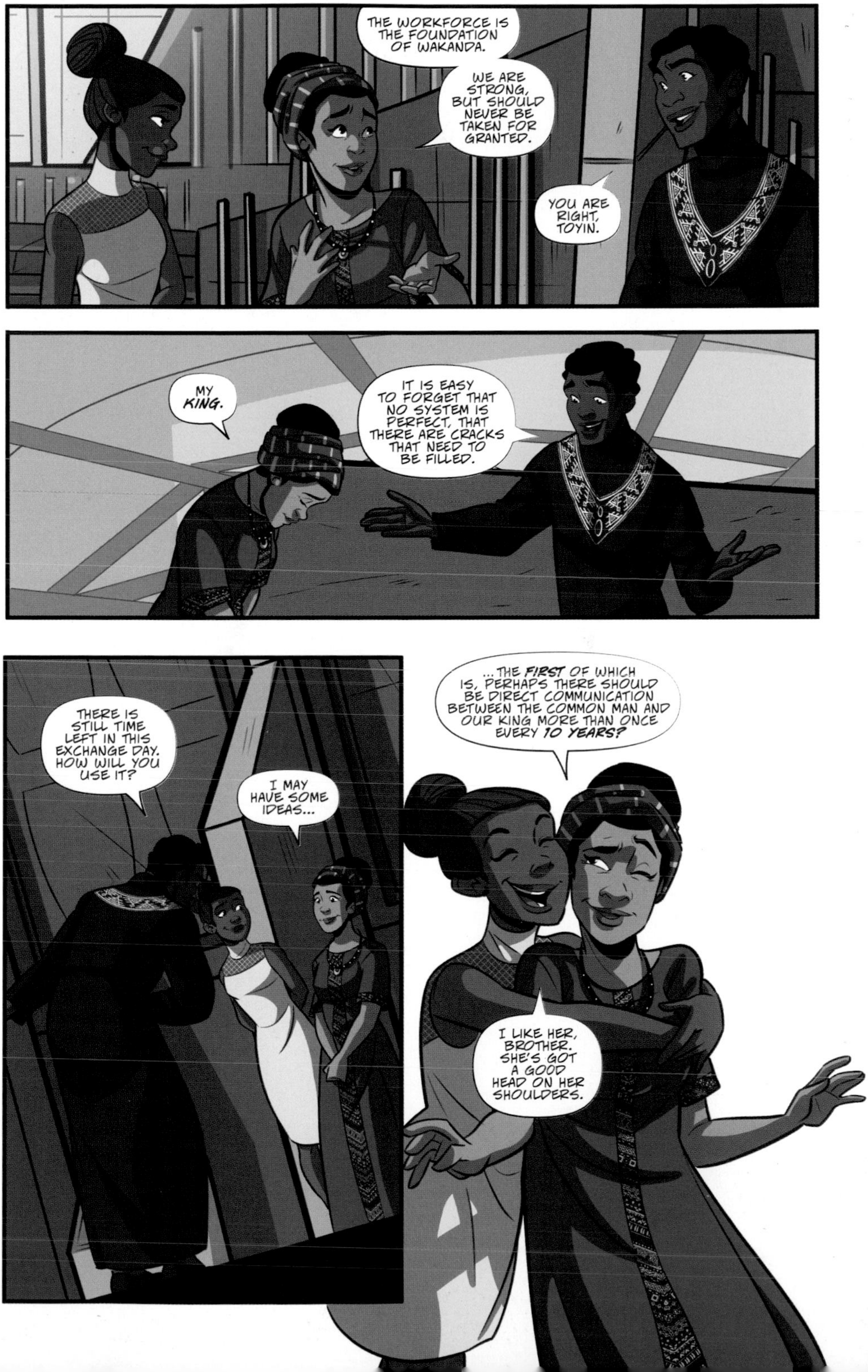
THE WORKFORCE IS THE FOUNDATION OF WAKANDA.
WE ARE STRONG, BUT SHOULD NEVER BE TAKEN FOR GRANTED.
YOU ARE RIGHT, TOYIN.
MY *KING*.
IT IS EASY TO FORGET THAT NO SYSTEM IS PERFECT, THAT THERE ARE CRACKS THAT NEED TO BE FILLED.
THERE IS STILL TIME LEFT IN THIS EXCHANGE DAY. HOW WILL YOU USE IT?
I MAY HAVE SOME IDEAS...
...THE *FIRST* OF WHICH IS, PERHAPS THERE SHOULD BE DIRECT COMMUNICATION BETWEEN THE COMMON MAN AND OUR KING MORE THAN ONCE EVERY *10 YEARS?*
I LIKE HER, BROTHER. SHE'S GOT A GOOD HEAD ON HER SHOULDERS.

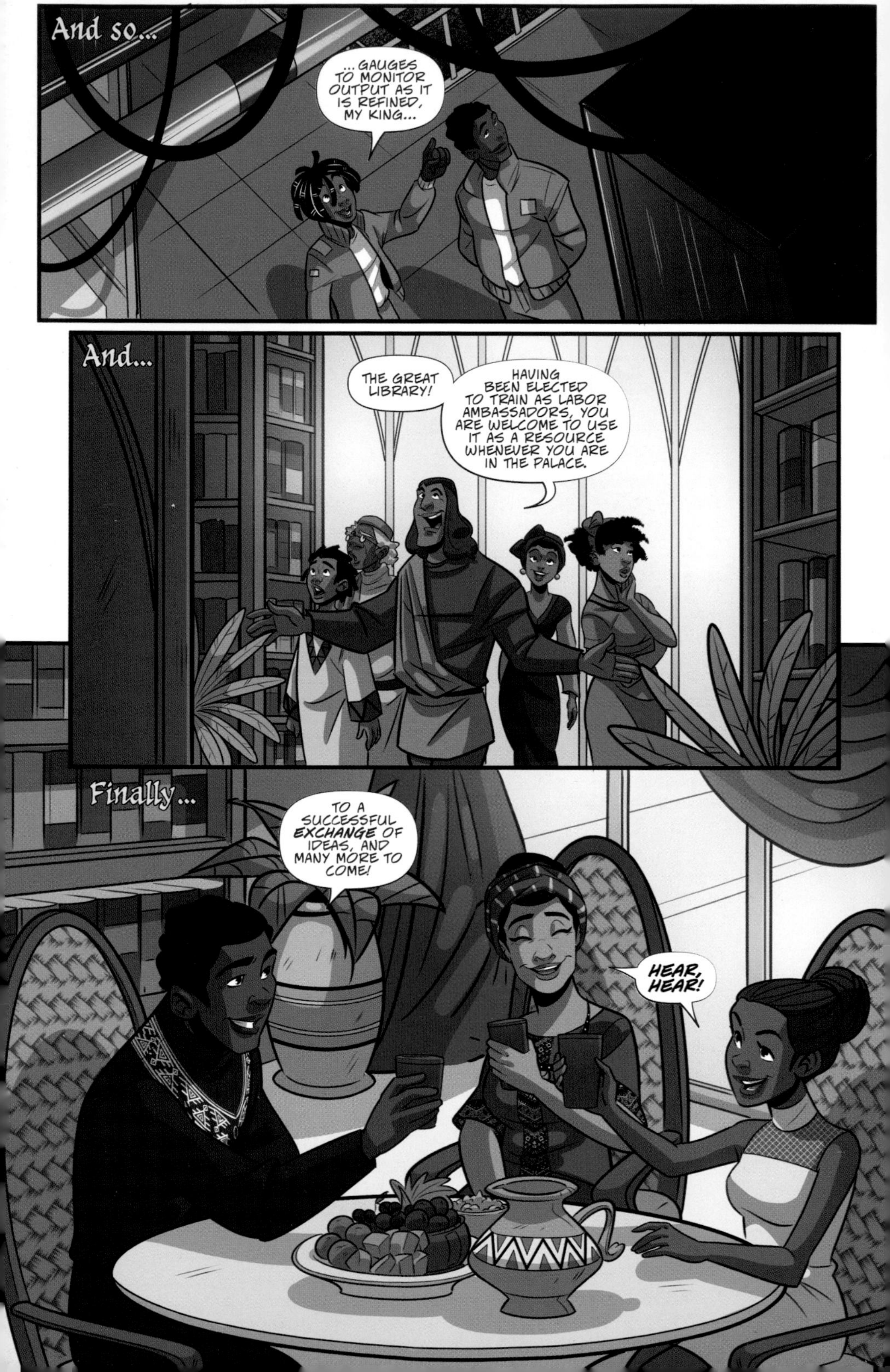
And so...
... GAUGES TO MONITOR OUTPUT AS IT IS REFINED, MY KING...
And...
THE GREAT LIBRARY!
HAVING BEEN ELECTED TO TRAIN AS LABOR AMBASSADORS, YOU ARE WELCOME TO USE IT AS A RESOURCE WHENEVER YOU ARE IN THE PALACE.
Finally...
TO A SUCCESSFUL EXCHANGE OF IDEAS, AND MANY MORE TO COME!
HEAR, HEAR!

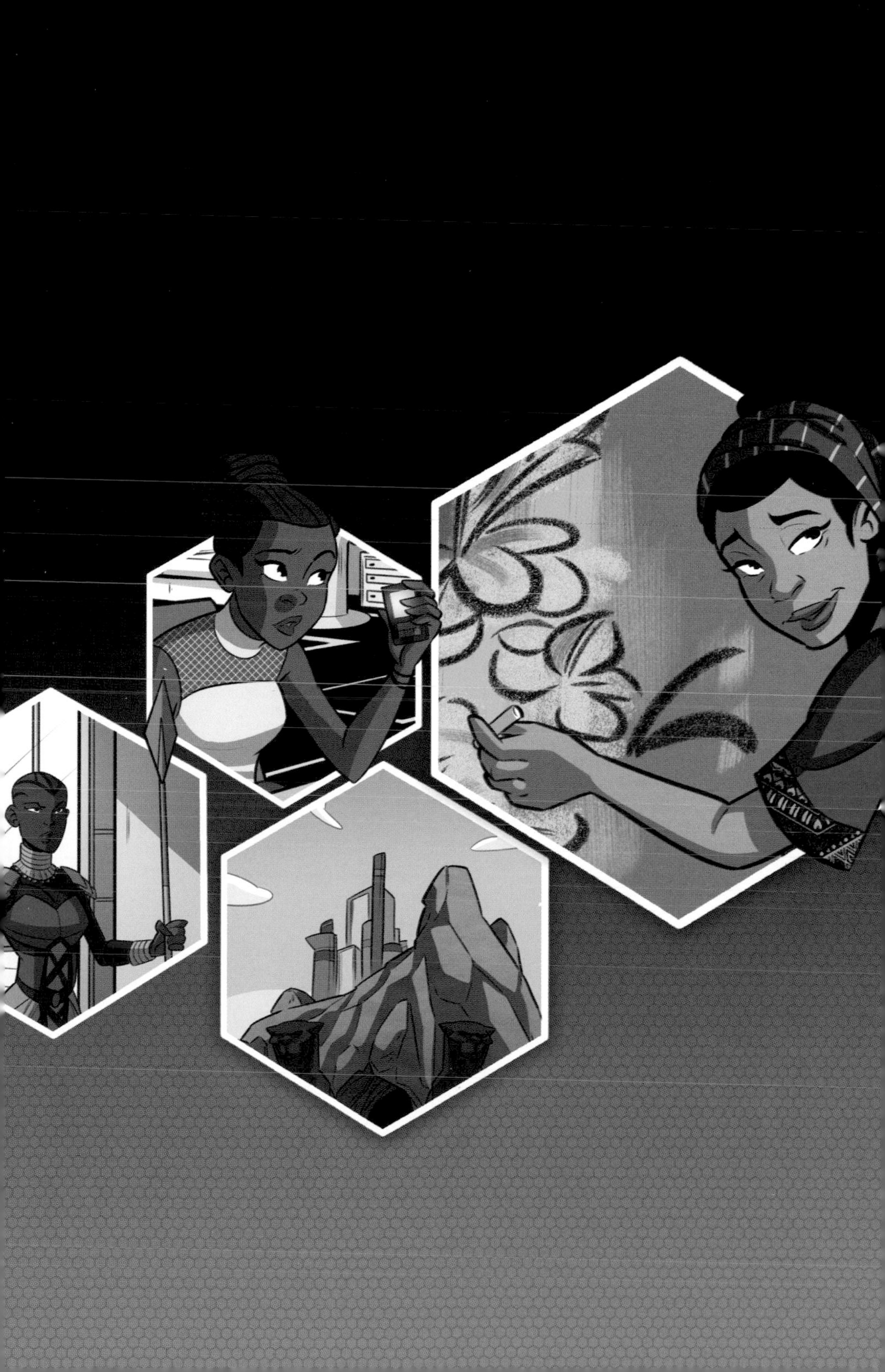

ART BY: ARIANNA FLOREAN

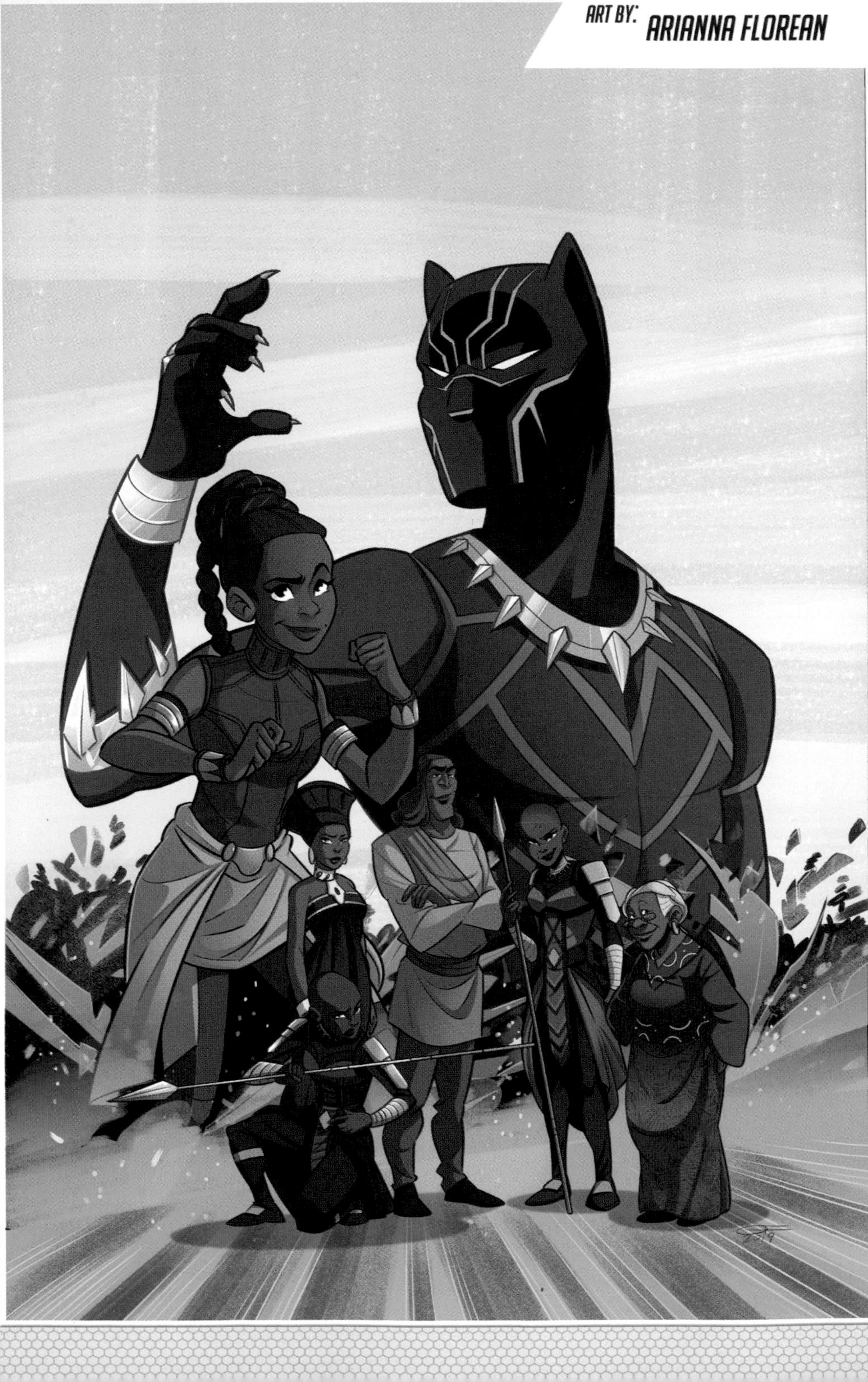

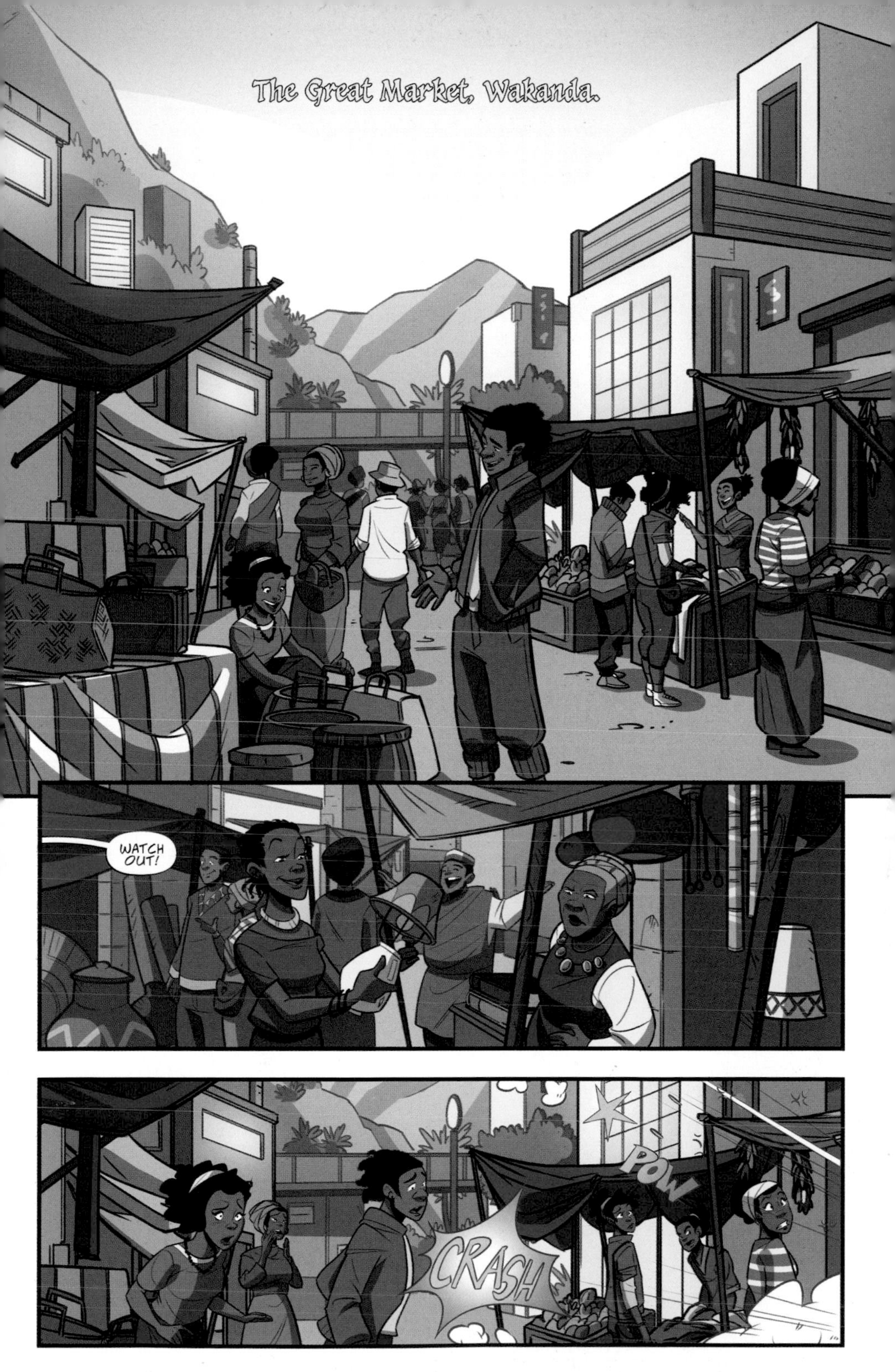
The Great Market, Wakanda.
WATCH OUT!
POW
CRASH

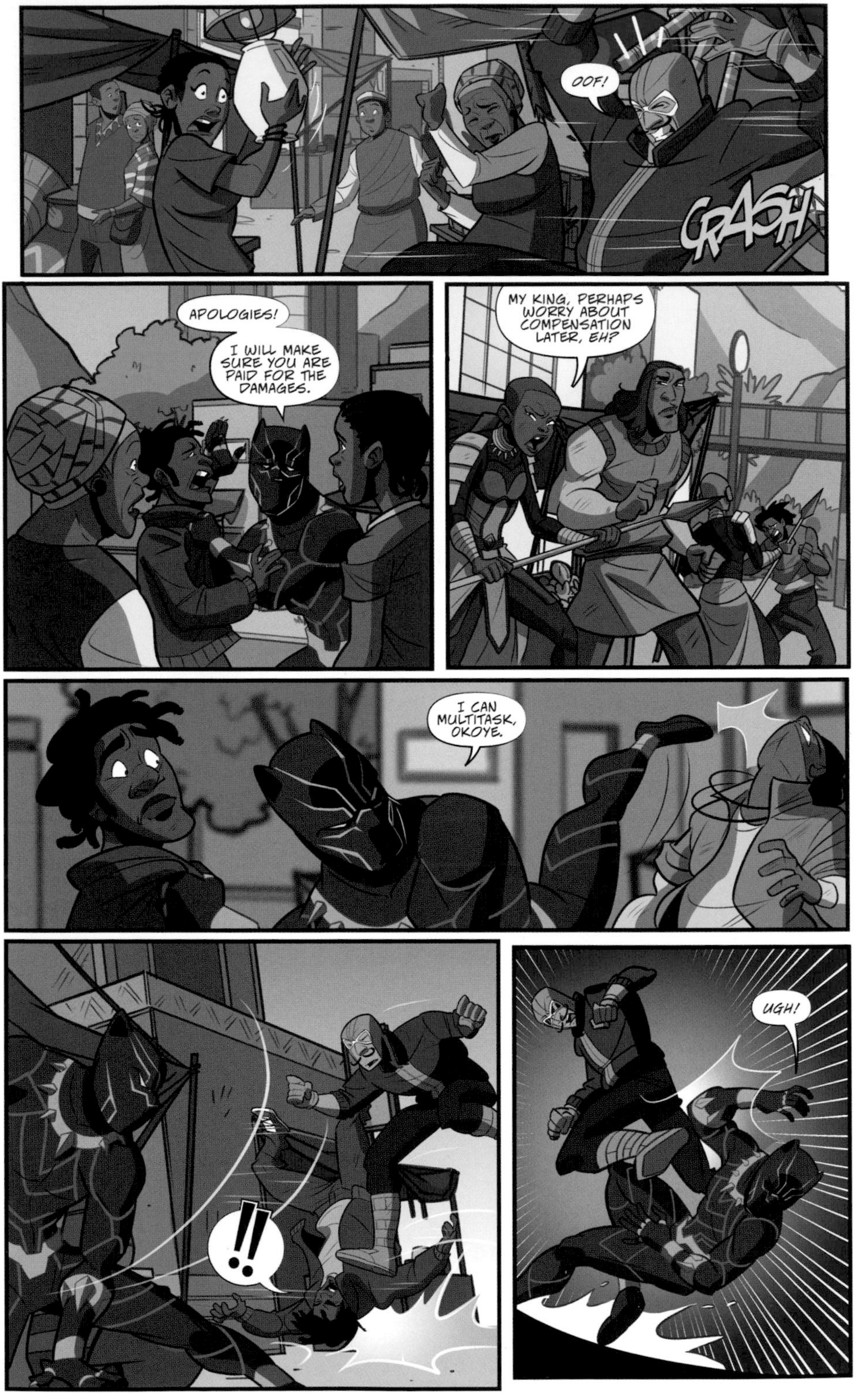
OOF!
CRASH
APOLOGIES!
I WILL MAKE SURE YOU ARE PAID FOR THE DAMAGES.
MY KING, PERHAPS WORRY ABOUT COMPENSATION LATER, EH?
I CAN MULTITASK, OKOYE.
!!
UGH!

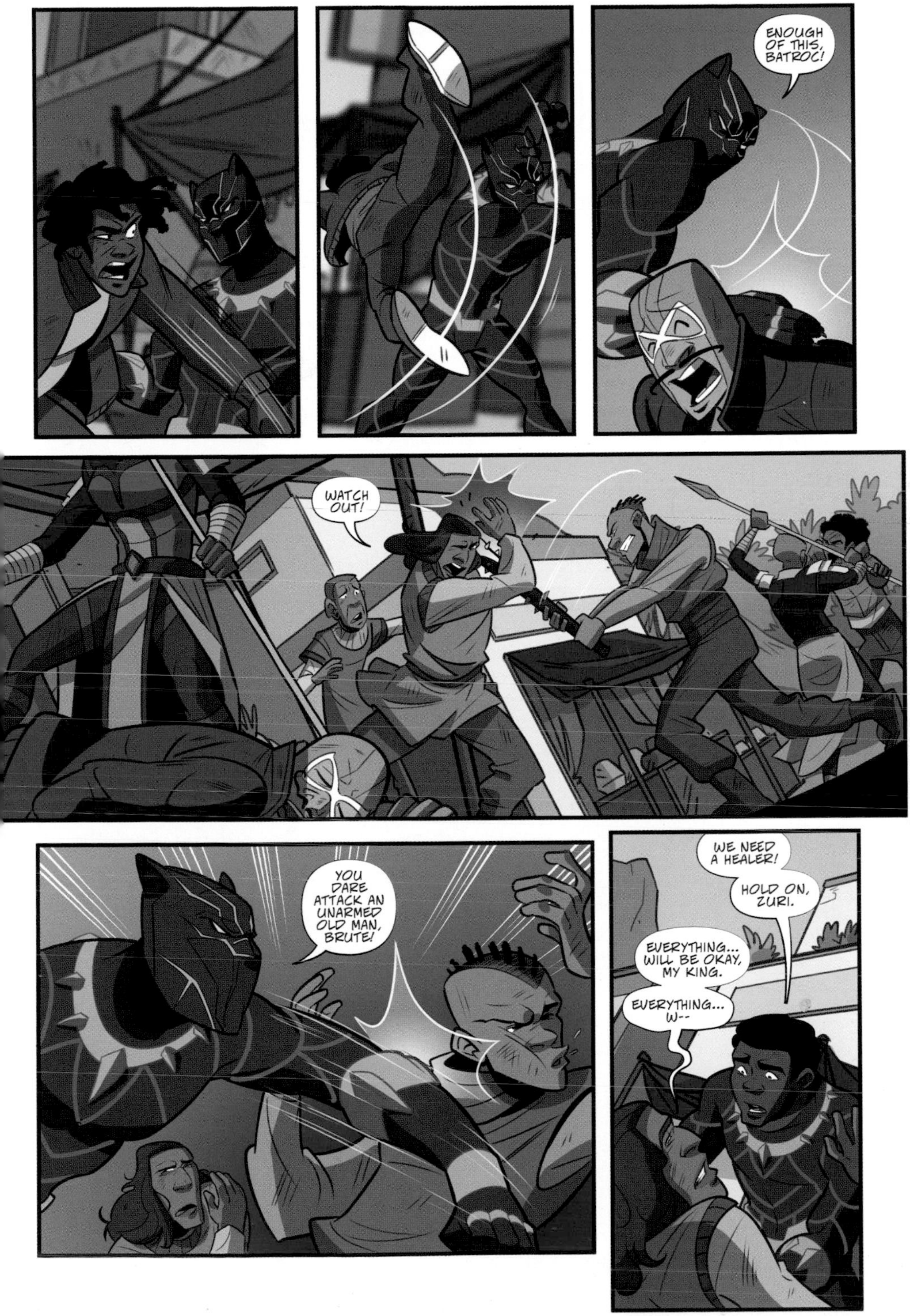
ENOUGH OF THIS, BATROC!
WATCH OUT!
YOU DARE ATTACK AN UNARMED OLD MAN, BRUTE!
WE NEED A HEALER!
HOLD ON, ZURI.
EVERYTHING... WILL BE OKAY, MY KING.
EVERYTHING... W--

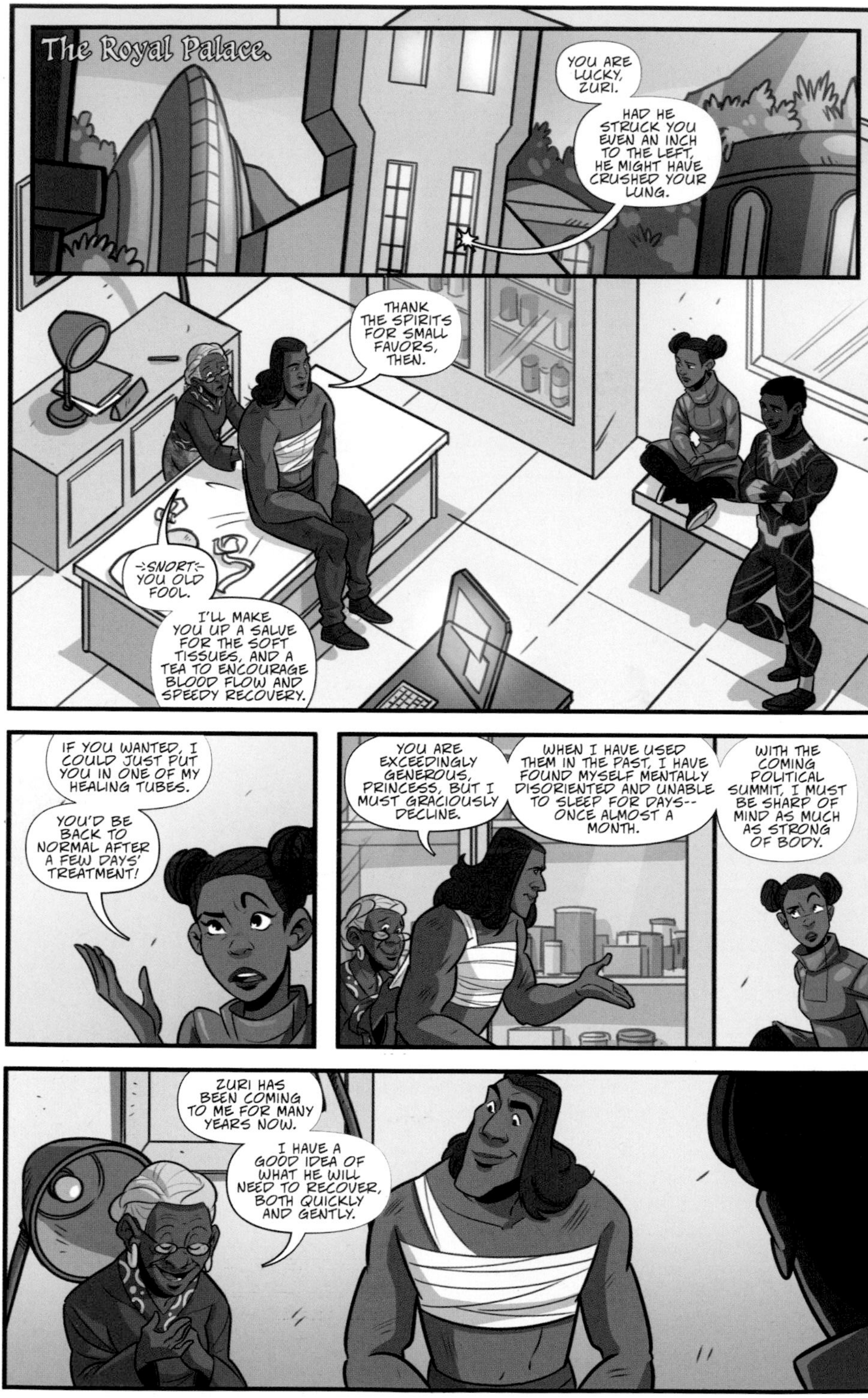
The Royal Palace.
YOU ARE LUCKY, ZURI.
HAD HE STRUCK YOU EVEN AN INCH TO THE LEFT, HE MIGHT HAVE CRUSHED YOUR LUNG.
THANK THE SPIRITS FOR SMALL FAVORS, THEN.
-SNORT- YOU OLD FOOL.
I'LL MAKE YOU UP A SALVE FOR THE SOFT TISSUES, AND A TEA TO ENCOURAGE BLOOD FLOW AND SPEEDY RECOVERY.
IF YOU WANTED, I COULD JUST PUT YOU IN ONE OF MY HEALING TUBES.
YOU'D BE BACK TO NORMAL AFTER A FEW DAYS' TREATMENT!
YOU ARE EXCEEDINGLY GENEROUS, PRINCESS, BUT I MUST GRACIOUSLY DECLINE.
WHEN I HAVE USED THEM IN THE PAST, I HAVE FOUND MYSELF MENTALLY DISORIENTED AND UNABLE TO SLEEP FOR DAYS-- ONCE ALMOST A MONTH.
WITH THE COMING POLITICAL SUMMIT, I MUST BE SHARP OF MIND AS MUCH AS STRONG OF BODY.
ZURI HAS BEEN COMING TO ME FOR MANY YEARS NOW.
I HAVE A GOOD IDEA OF WHAT HE WILL NEED TO RECOVER, BOTH QUICKLY AND GENTLY.

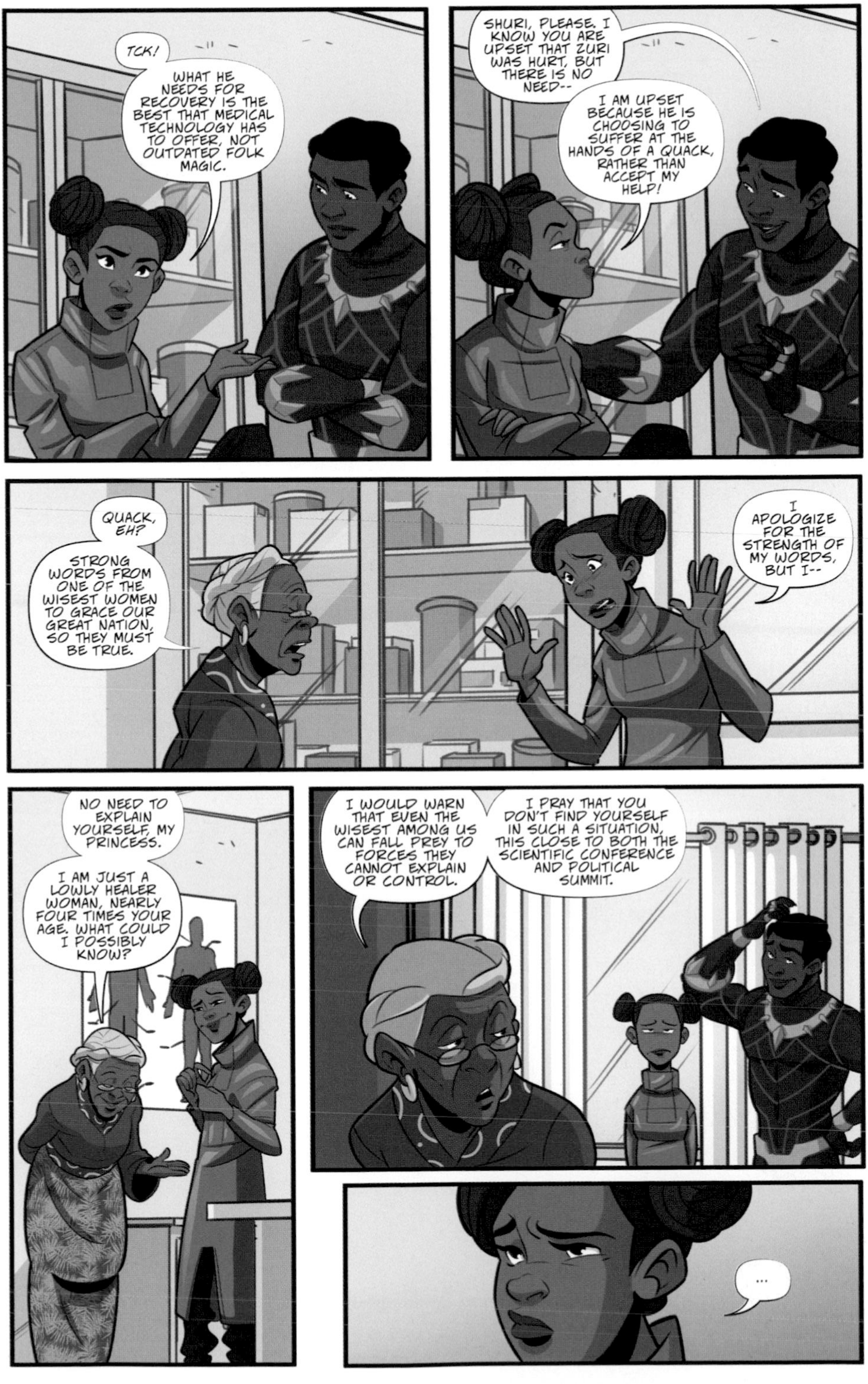
TCK!
WHAT HE NEEDS FOR RECOVERY IS THE BEST THAT MEDICAL TECHNOLOGY HAS TO OFFER, NOT OUTDATED FOLK MAGIC.
SHURI, PLEASE. I KNOW YOU ARE UPSET THAT ZURI WAS HURT, BUT THERE IS NO NEED--
I AM UPSET BECAUSE HE IS CHOOSING TO SUFFER AT THE HANDS OF A QUACK, RATHER THAN ACCEPT MY HELP!
QUACK, EH?
STRONG WORDS FROM ONE OF THE WISEST WOMEN TO GRACE OUR GREAT NATION, SO THEY MUST BE TRUE.
I APOLOGIZE FOR THE STRENGTH OF MY WORDS, BUT I--
NO NEED TO EXPLAIN YOURSELF, MY PRINCESS.
I AM JUST A LOWLY HEALER WOMAN, NEARLY FOUR TIMES YOUR AGE. WHAT COULD I POSSIBLY KNOW?
I WOULD WARN THAT EVEN THE WISEST AMONG US CAN FALL PREY TO FORCES THEY CANNOT EXPLAIN OR CONTROL.
I PRAY THAT YOU DON'T FIND YOURSELF IN SUCH A SITUATION, THIS CLOSE TO BOTH THE SCIENTIFIC CONFERENCE AND POLITICAL SUMMIT.
...

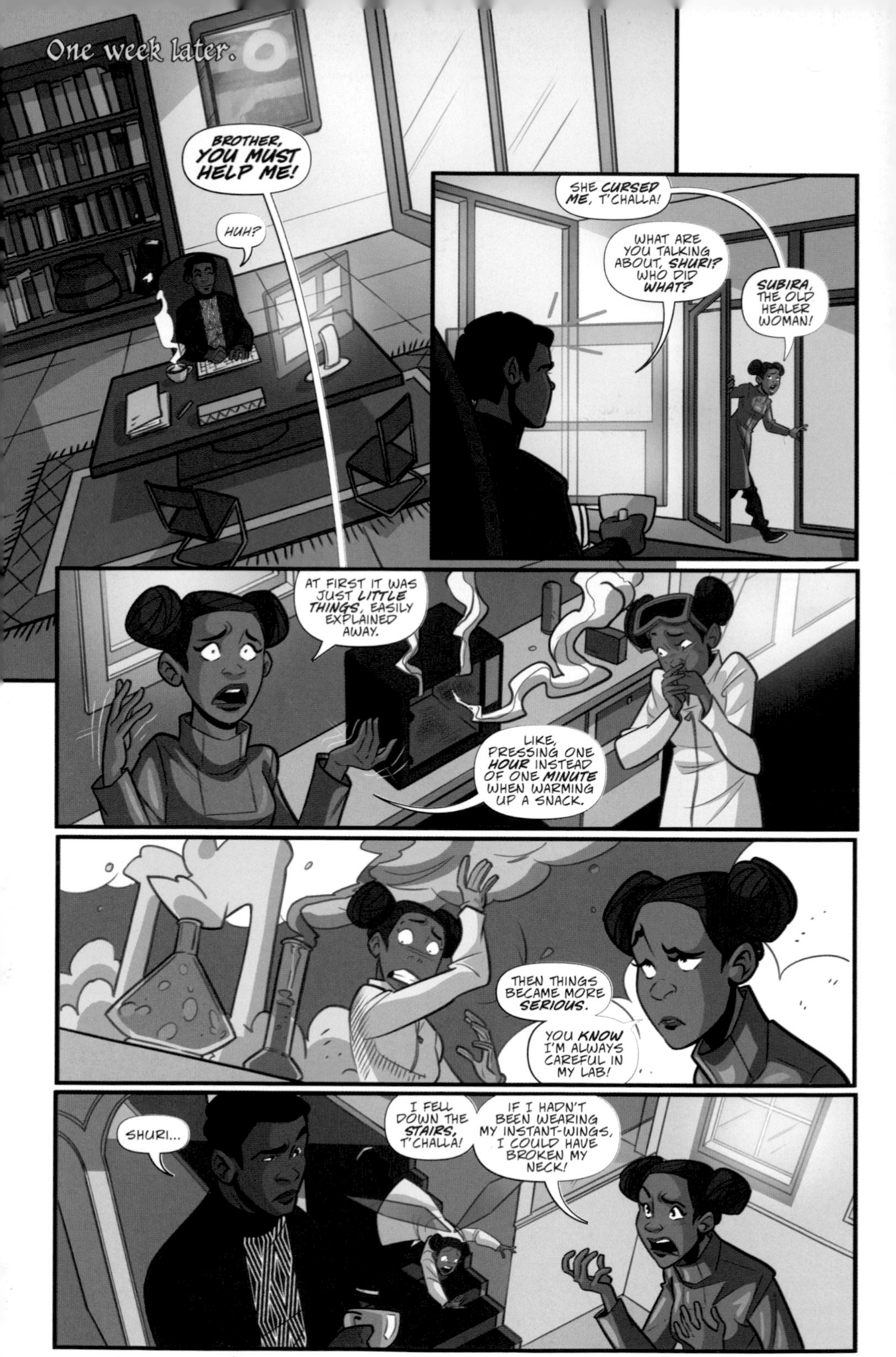

One week later.
BROTHER, YOU MUST HELP ME!
HUH?
SHE CURSED ME, T'CHALLA!
WHAT ARE YOU TALKING ABOUT, SHURI? WHO DID WHAT?
SUBIRA, THE OLD HEALER WOMAN!
AT FIRST IT WAS JUST LITTLE THINGS, EASILY EXPLAINED AWAY.
LIKE, PRESSING ONE HOUR INSTEAD OF ONE MINUTE WHEN WARMING UP A SNACK.
THEN THINGS BECAME MORE SERIOUS.
YOU KNOW I'M ALWAYS CAREFUL IN MY LAB!
SHURI...
I FELL DOWN THE STAIRS, T'CHALLA!
IF I HADN'T BEEN WEARING MY INSTANT-WINGS, I COULD HAVE BROKEN MY NECK!

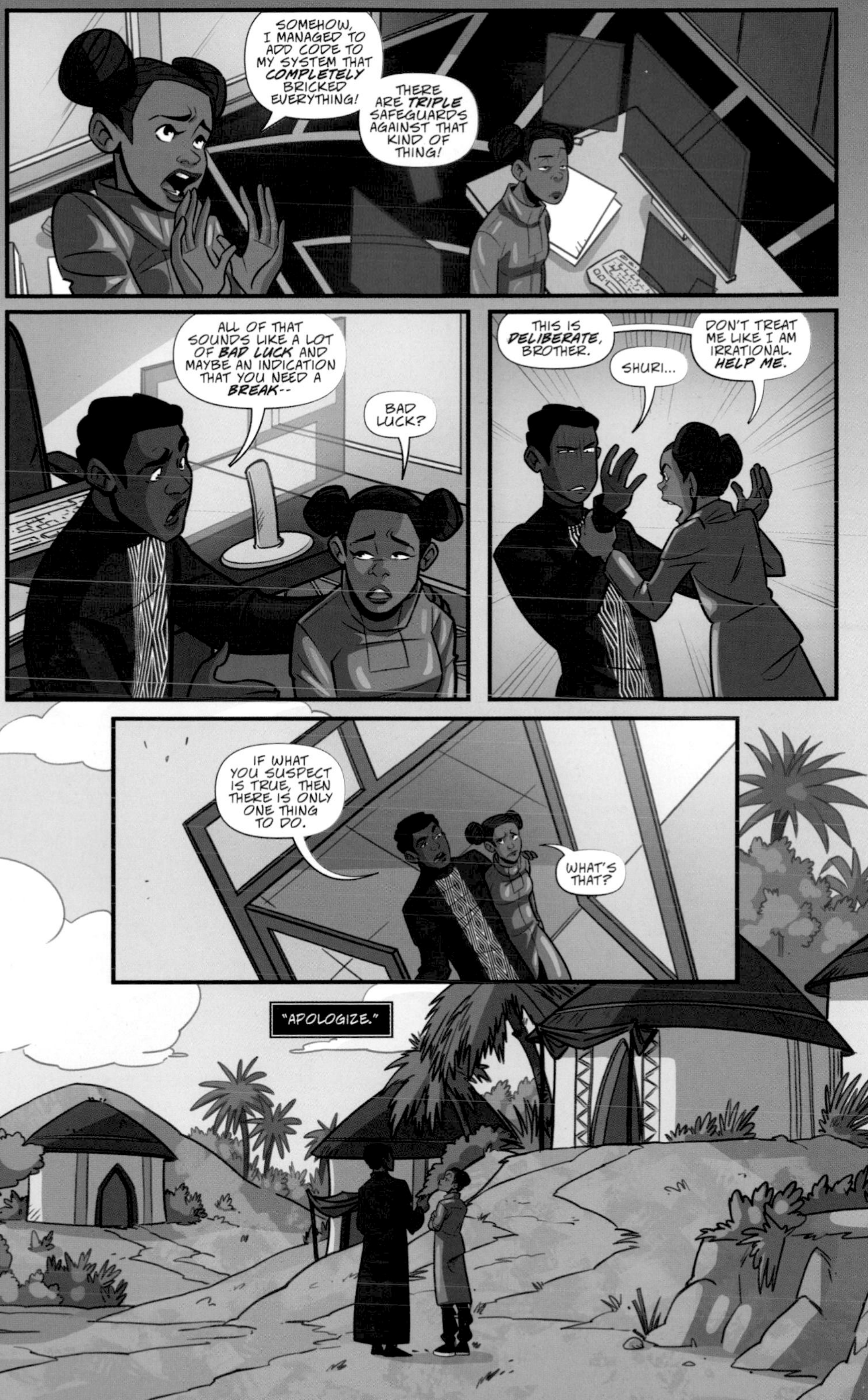
SOMEHOW, I MANAGED TO ADD CODE TO MY SYSTEM THAT COMPLETELY BRICKED EVERYTHING!
THERE ARE TRIPLE SAFEGUARDS AGAINST THAT KIND OF THING!
ALL OF THAT SOUNDS LIKE A LOT OF BAD LUCK AND MAYBE AN INDICATION THAT YOU NEED A BREAK--
BAD LUCK?
THIS IS DELIBERATE, BROTHER.
SHURI...
DON'T TREAT ME LIKE I AM IRRATIONAL. HELP ME.
IF WHAT YOU SUSPECT IS TRUE, THEN THERE IS ONLY ONE THING TO DO.
WHAT'S THAT?
"APOLOGIZE."

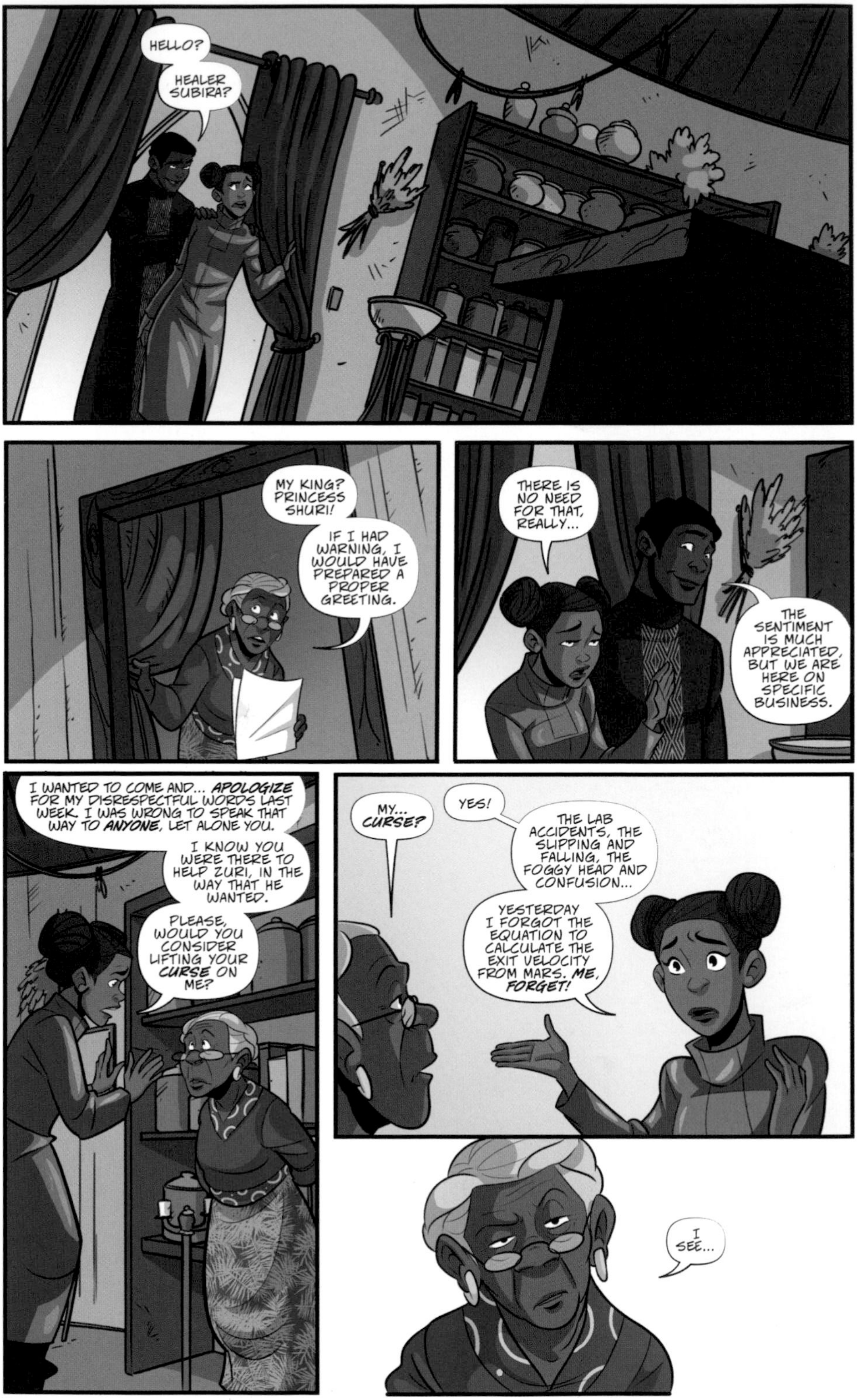
HELLO?
HEALER SUBIRA?
MY KING? PRINCESS SHURI!
IF I HAD WARNING, I WOULD HAVE PREPARED A PROPER GREETING.
THERE IS NO NEED FOR THAT, REALLY...
THE SENTIMENT IS MUCH APPRECIATED, BUT WE ARE HERE ON SPECIFIC BUSINESS.
I WANTED TO COME AND... APOLOGIZE FOR MY DISRESPECTFUL WORDS LAST WEEK. I WAS WRONG TO SPEAK THAT WAY TO ANYONE, LET ALONE YOU.
I KNOW YOU WERE THERE TO HELP ZURI, IN THE WAY THAT HE WANTED.
PLEASE, WOULD YOU CONSIDER LIFTING YOUR CURSE ON ME?
MY... CURSE?
YES!
THE LAB ACCIDENTS, THE SLIPPING AND FALLING, THE FOGGY HEAD AND CONFUSION...
YESTERDAY I FORGOT THE EQUATION TO CALCULATE THE EXIT VELOCITY FROM MARS. ME, FORGET!
I SEE...

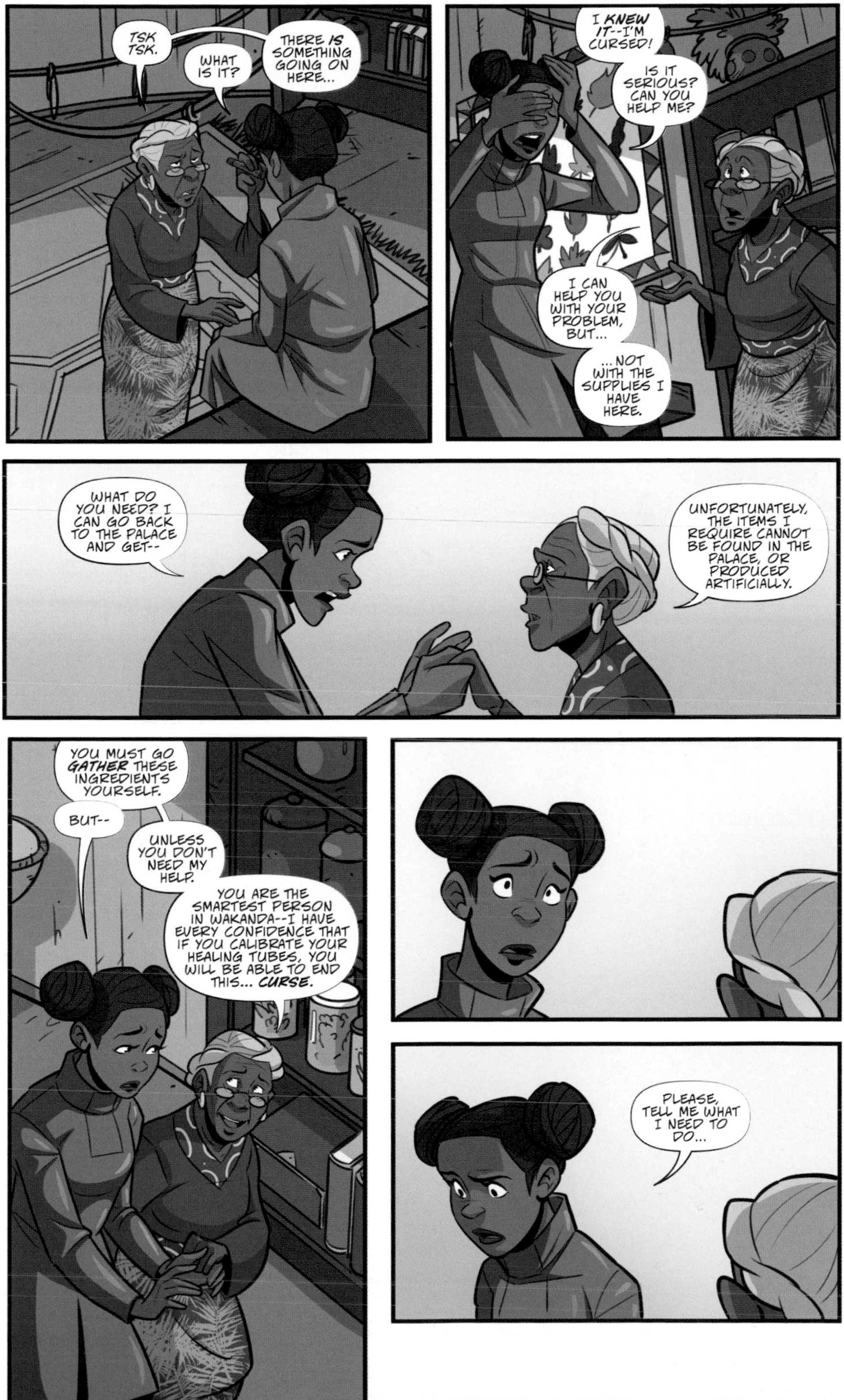
TSK TSK.
WHAT IS IT?
THERE IS SOMETHING GOING ON HERE...
I KNEW IT--I'M CURSED!
IS IT SERIOUS? CAN YOU HELP ME?
I CAN HELP YOU WITH YOUR PROBLEM, BUT...
...NOT WITH THE SUPPLIES I HAVE HERE.
WHAT DO YOU NEED? I CAN GO BACK TO THE PALACE AND GET--
UNFORTUNATELY, THE ITEMS I REQUIRE CANNOT BE FOUND IN THE PALACE, OR PRODUCED ARTIFICIALLY.
YOU MUST GO GATHER THESE INGREDIENTS YOURSELF.
BUT--
UNLESS YOU DON'T NEED MY HELP.
YOU ARE THE SMARTEST PERSON IN WAKANDA--I HAVE EVERY CONFIDENCE THAT IF YOU CALIBRATE YOUR HEALING TUBES, YOU WILL BE ABLE TO END THIS... CURSE.
PLEASE, TELL ME WHAT I NEED TO DO...

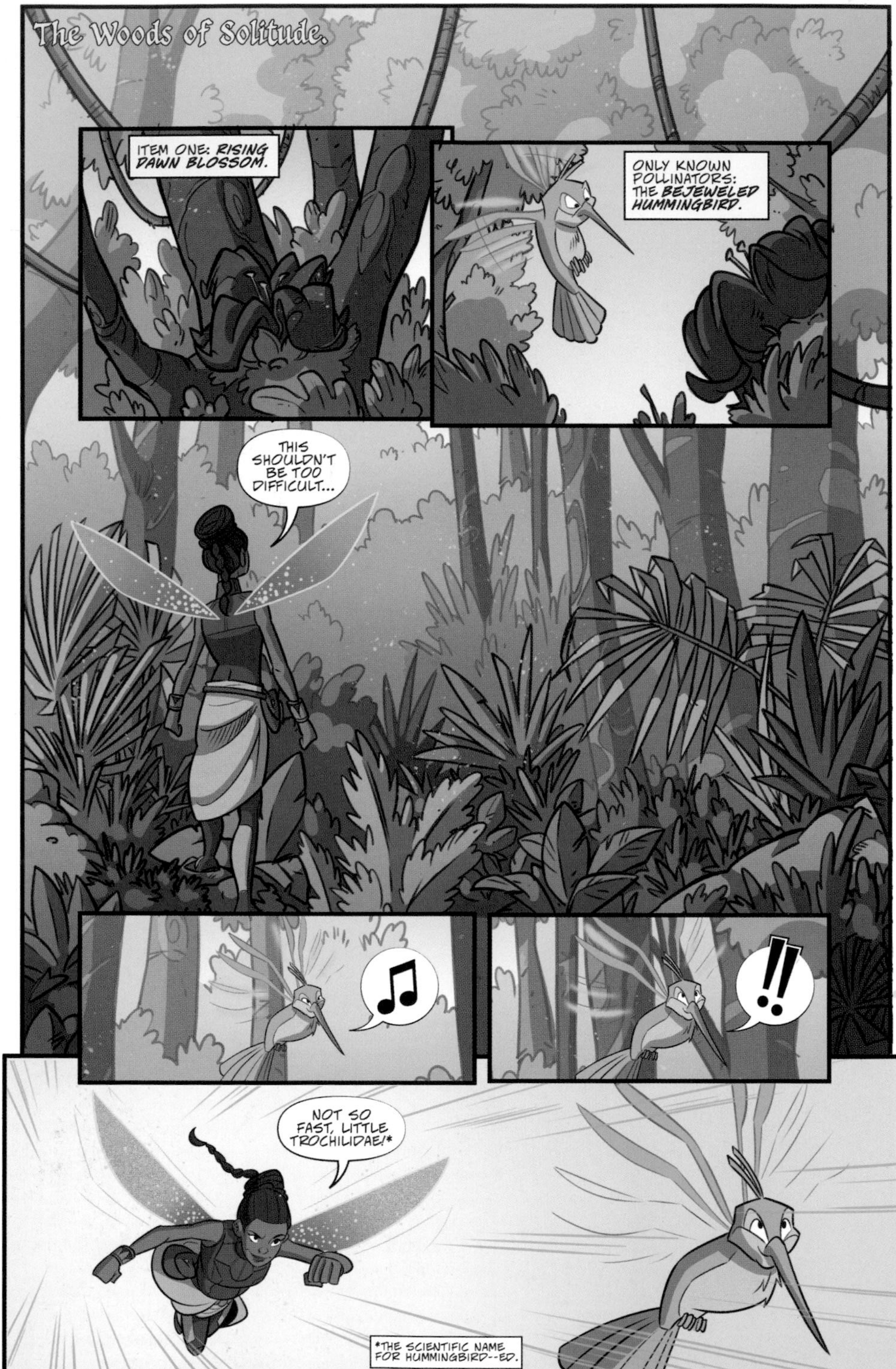
The Woods of Solitude.
ITEM ONE: RISING DAWN BLOSSOM.
ONLY KNOWN POLLINATORS: THE BEJEWELED HUMMINGBIRD.
THIS SHOULDN'T BE TOO DIFFICULT...
!!
NOT SO FAST, LITTLE TROCHILIDAE!*
*THE SCIENTIFIC NAME FOR HUMMINGBIRD--ED.

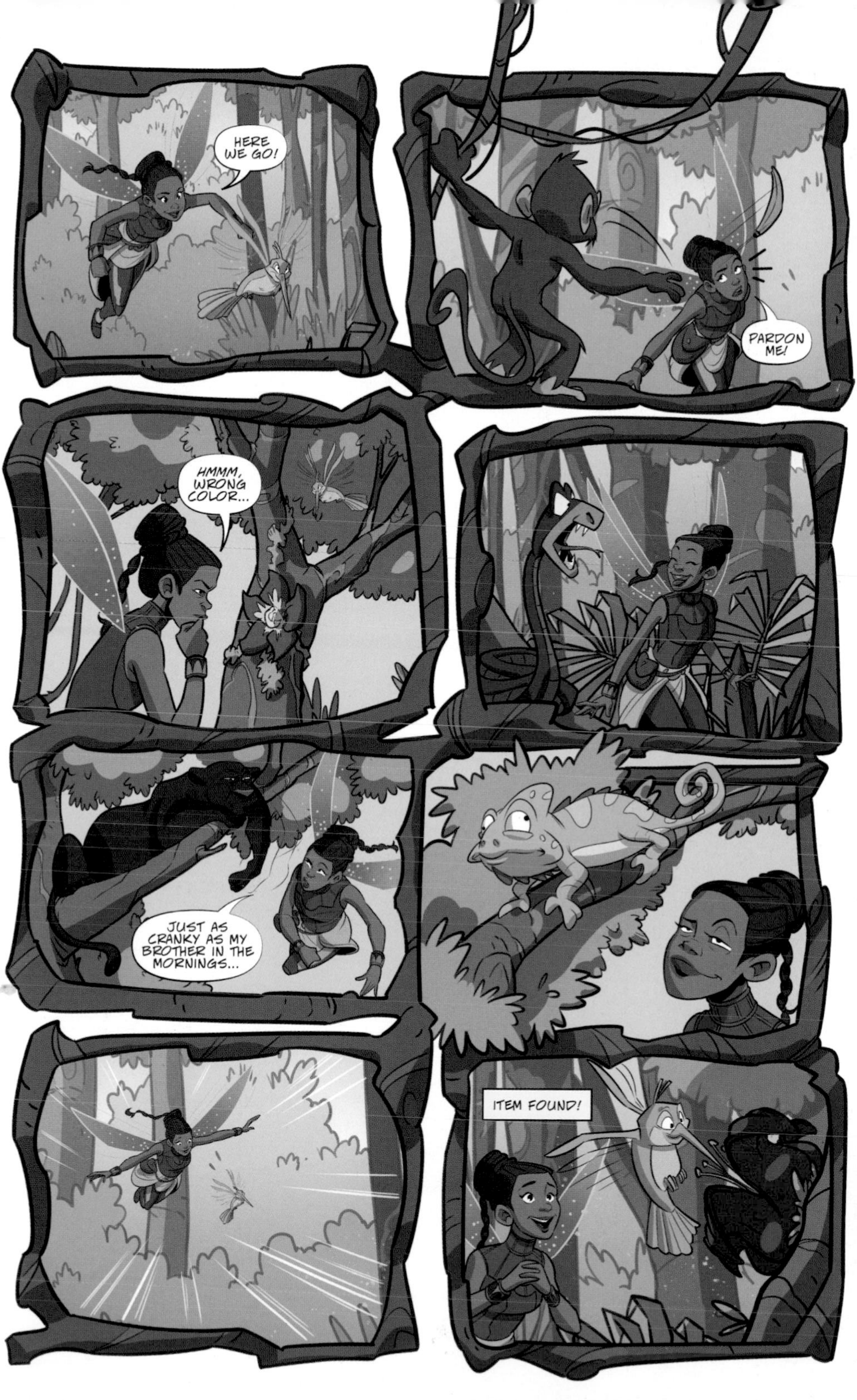
HERE WE GO!
PARDON ME!
HMMM, WRONG COLOR...
JUST AS CRANKY AS MY BROTHER IN THE MORNINGS...
ITEM FOUND!

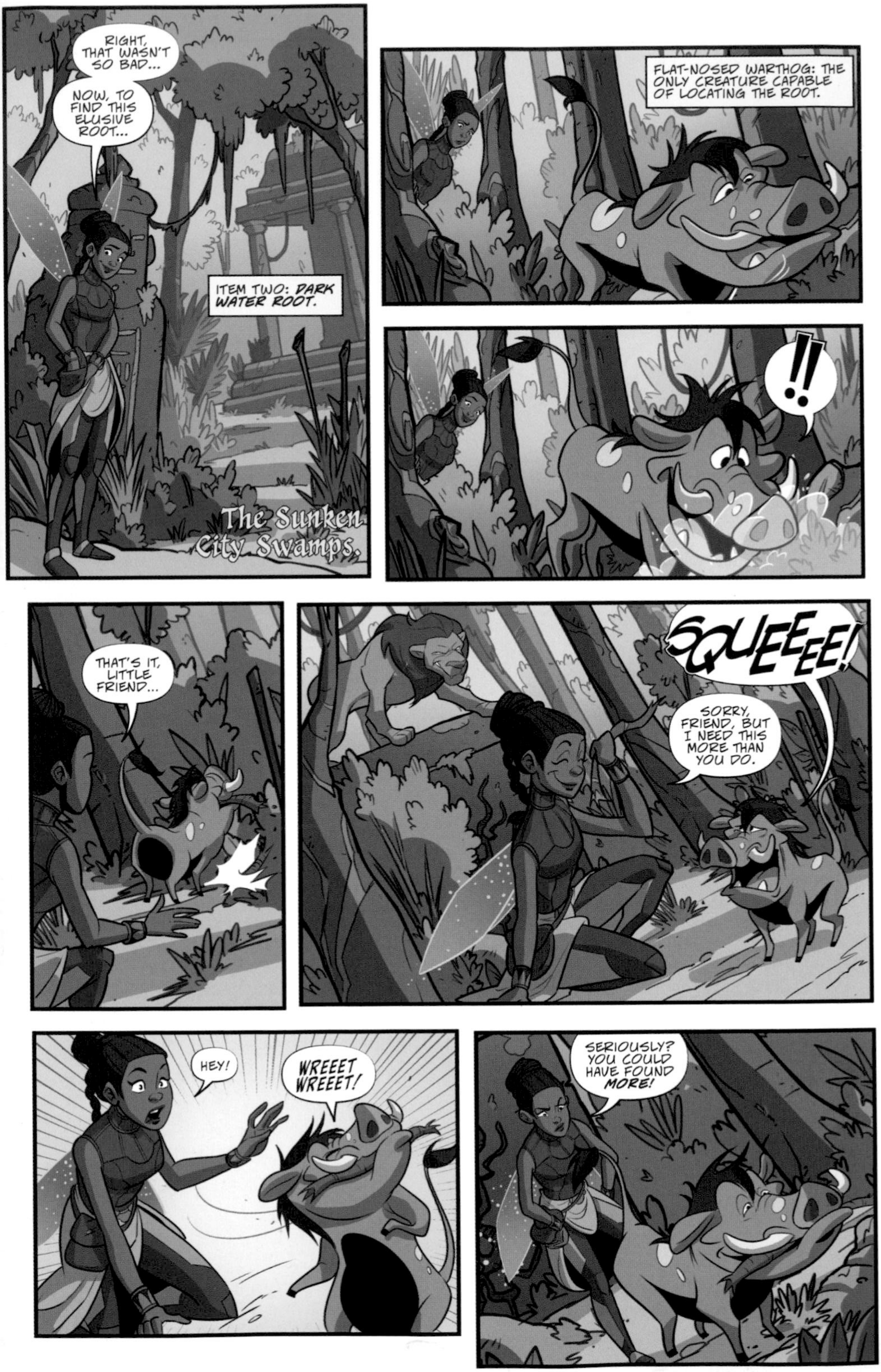
RIGHT, THAT WASN'T SO BAD...
NOW, TO FIND THIS ELUSIVE ROOT...
ITEM TWO: DARK WATER ROOT.
The Sunken City Swamps.
FLAT-NOSED WARTHOG: THE ONLY CREATURE CAPABLE OF LOCATING THE ROOT.
!!
THAT'S IT, LITTLE FRIEND...
SQUEEEEE!
SORRY, FRIEND, BUT I NEED THIS MORE THAN YOU DO.
HEY!
WREEET WREEET!
SERIOUSLY? YOU COULD HAVE FOUND MORE!

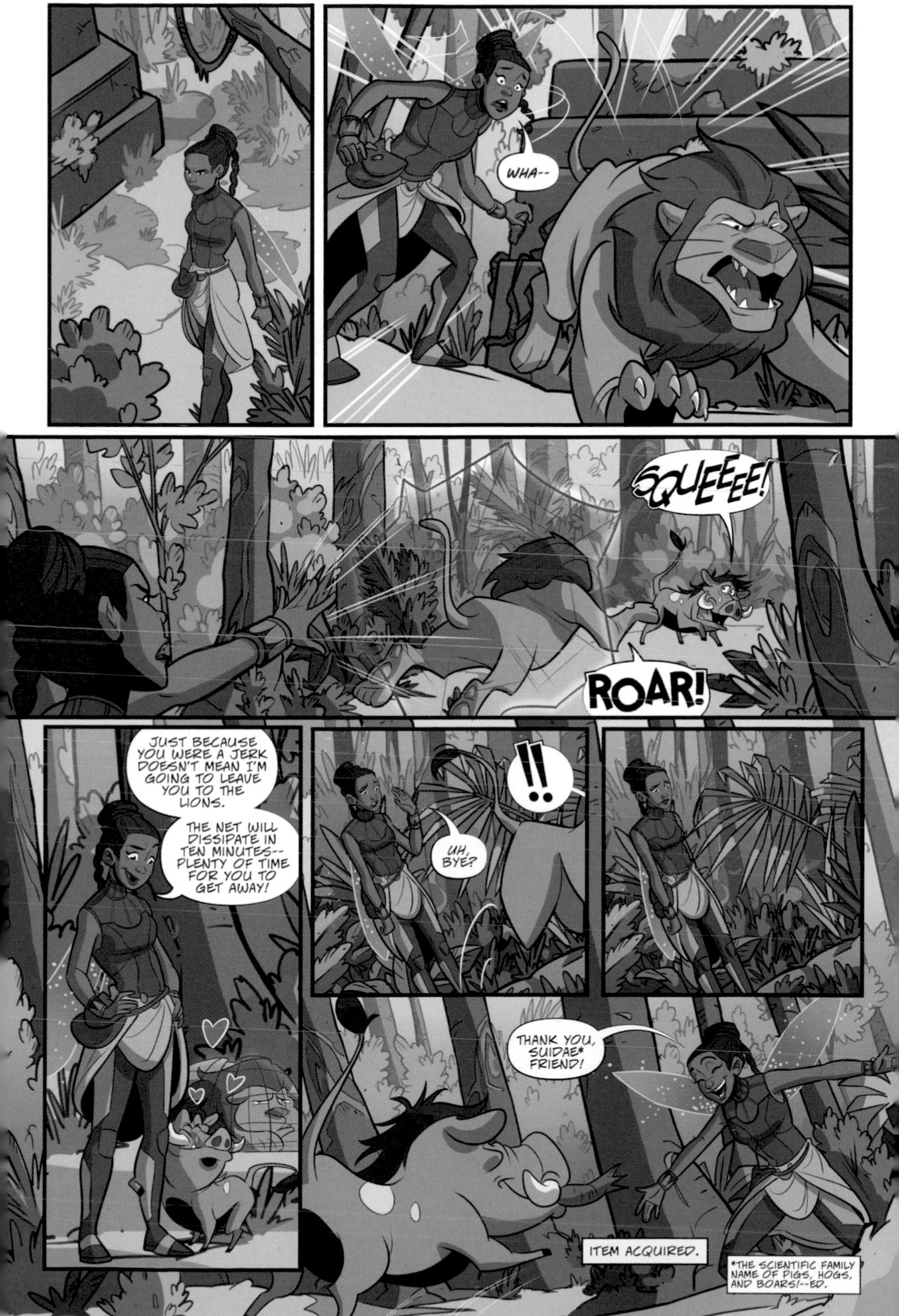
WHA--
SQUEEEEE!
ROAR!
JUST BECAUSE YOU WERE A JERK DOESN'T MEAN I'M GOING TO LEAVE YOU TO THE LIONS.
THE NET WILL DISSIPATE IN TEN MINUTES-- PLENTY OF TIME FOR YOU TO GET AWAY!
UH, BYE?
!!
THANK YOU, SUIDAE* FRIEND!
ITEM ACQUIRED.
*THE SCIENTIFIC FAMILY NAME OF PIGS, HOGS, AND BOARS!--ED.

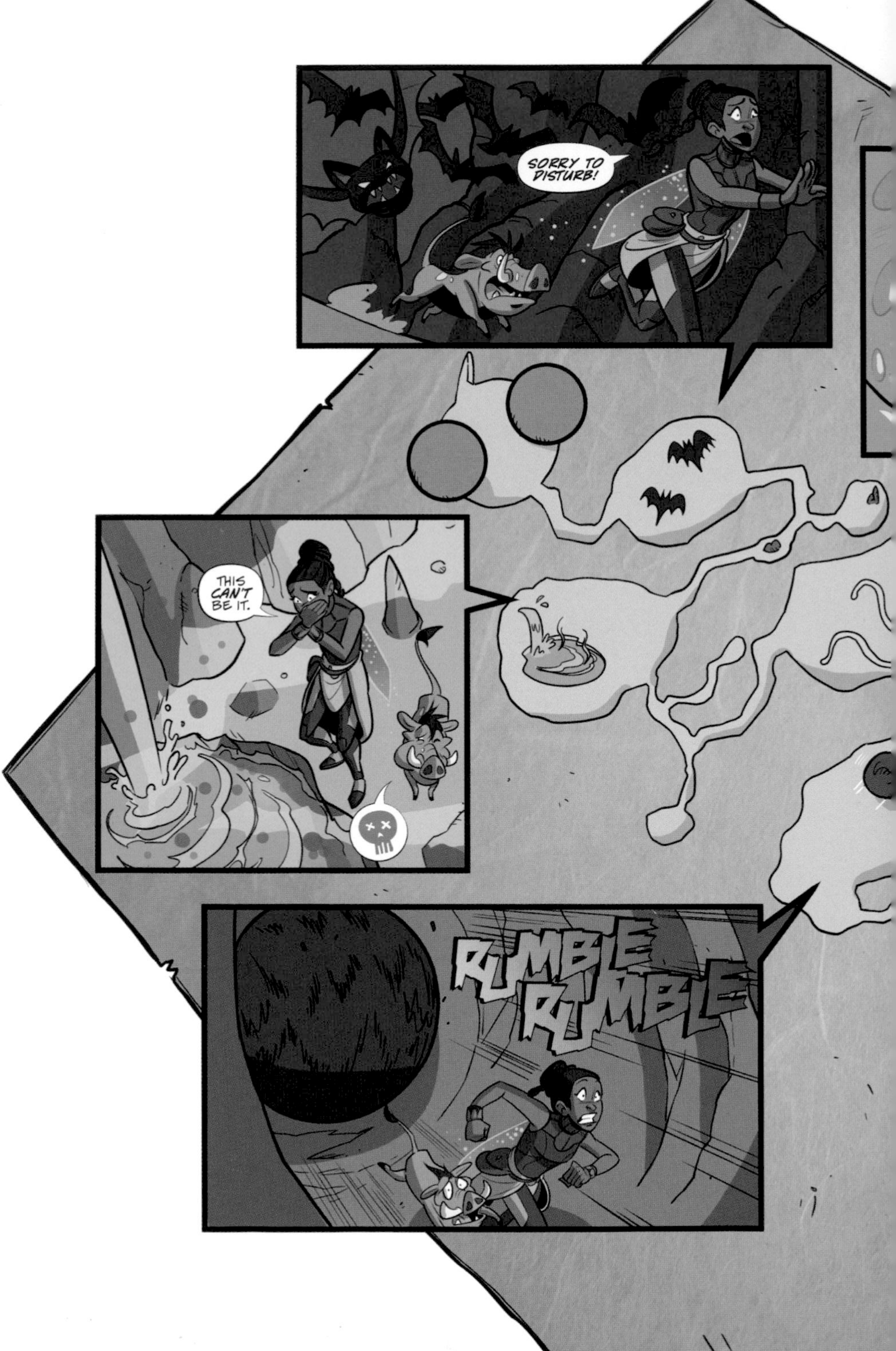
SORRY TO DISTURB!
THIS CAN'T BE IT.
RUMBLE RUMBLE

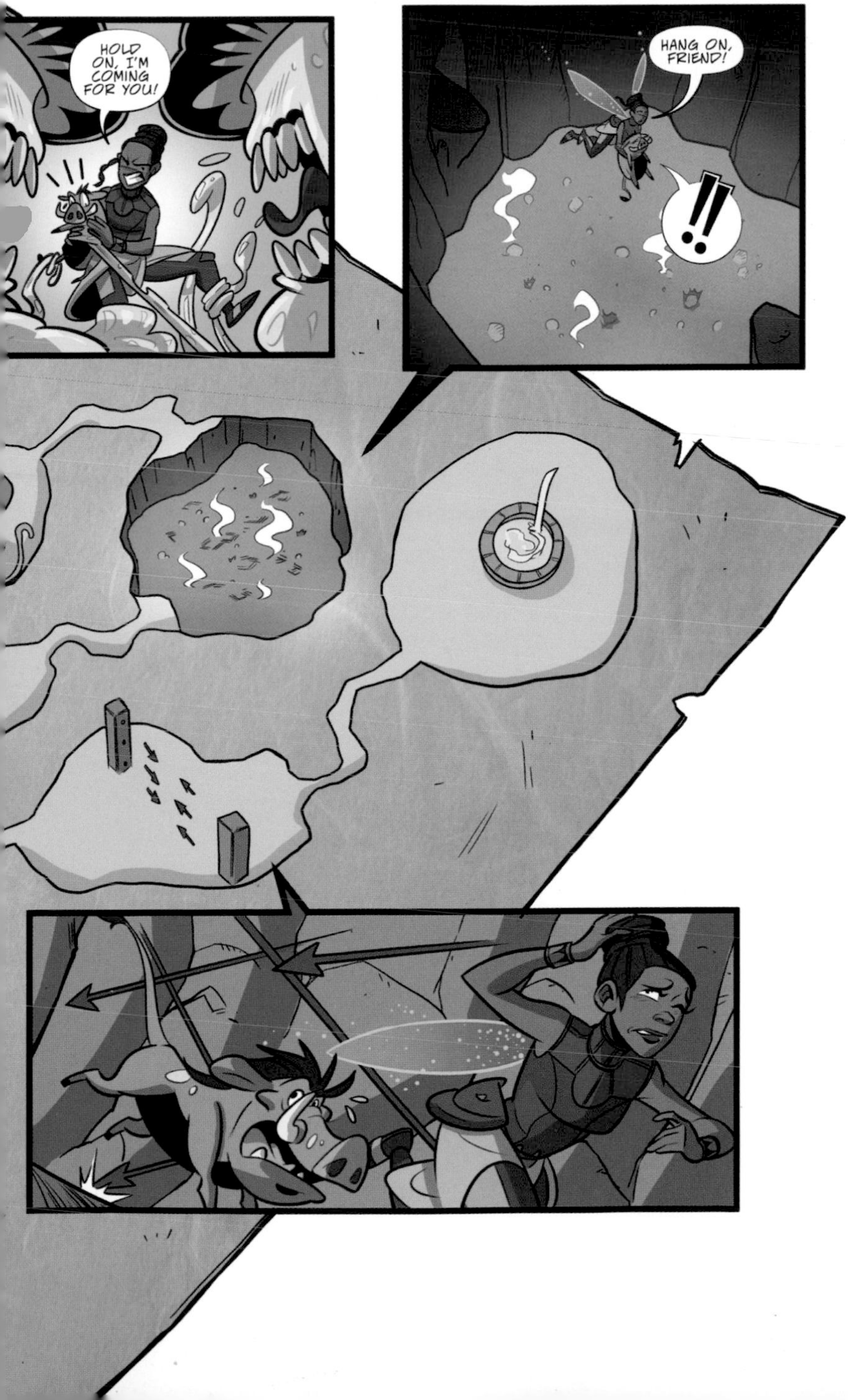
HOLD ON, I'M COMING FOR YOU!
HANG ON, FRIEND!
!!

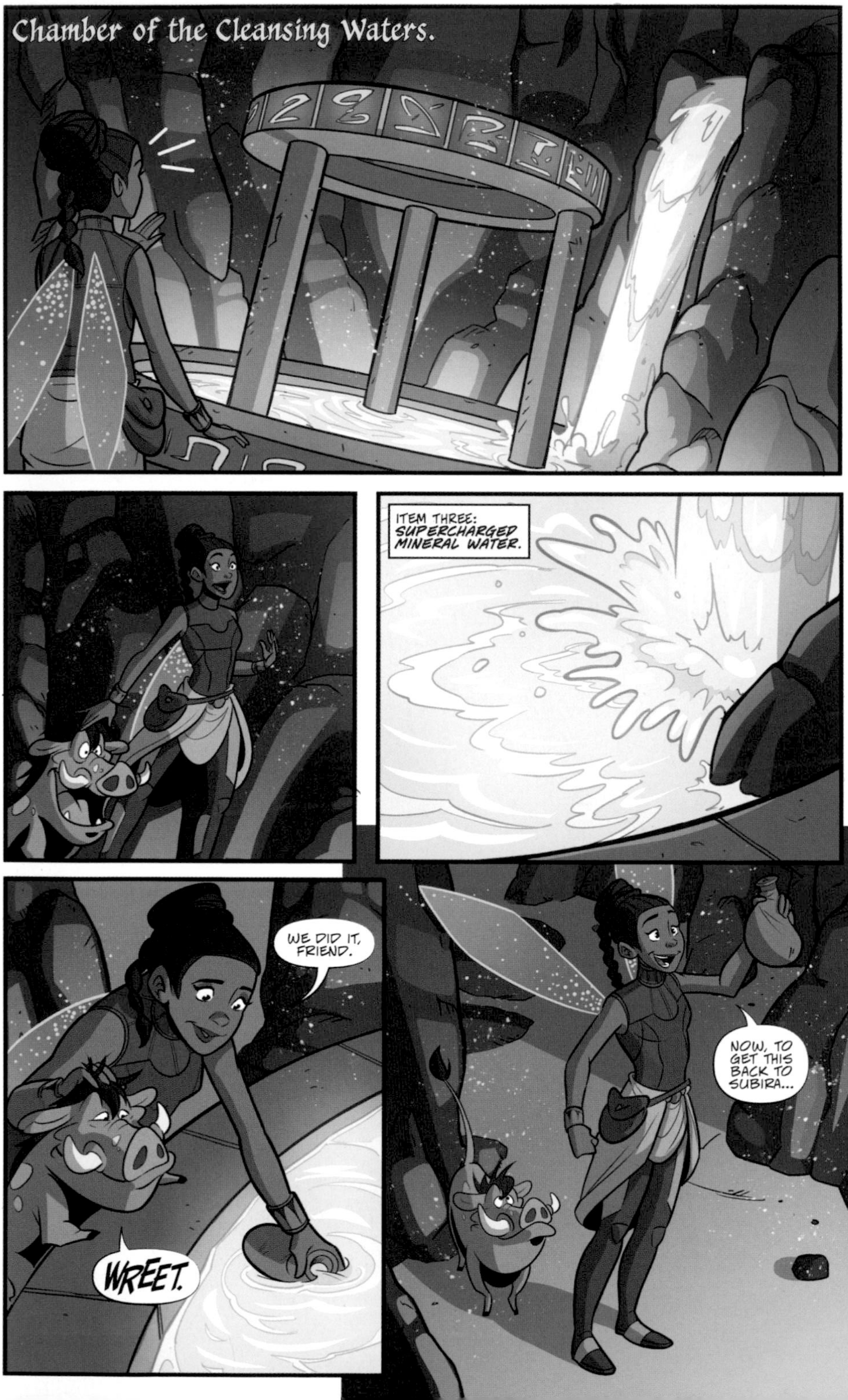

Chamber of the Cleansing Waters.
ITEM THREE: SUPERCHARGED MINERAL WATER.
WE DID IT, FRIEND.
WREET.
NOW, TO GET THIS BACK TO SUBIRA...

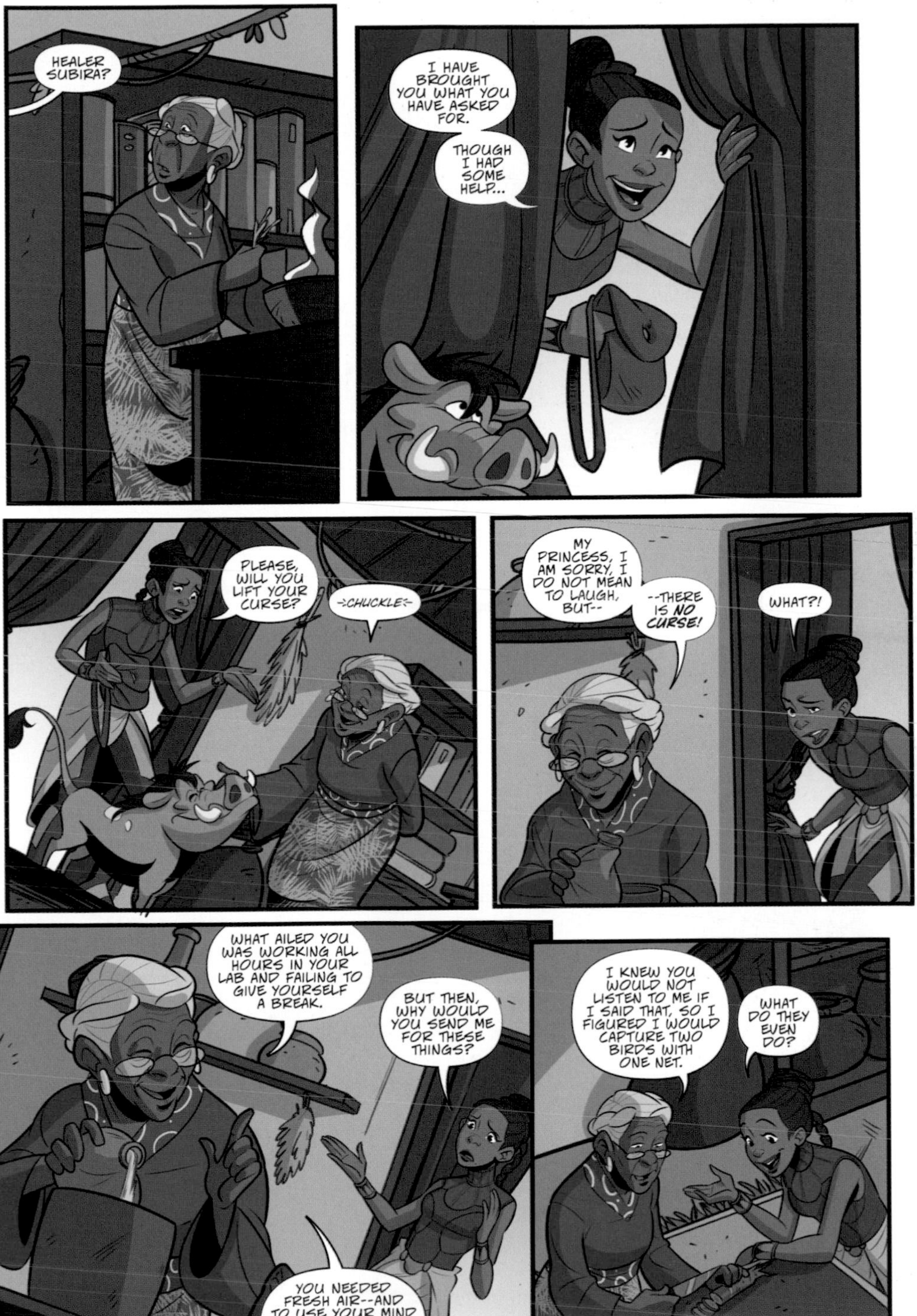
HEALER SUBIRA?
I HAVE BROUGHT YOU WHAT YOU HAVE ASKED FOR.
THOUGH I HAD SOME HELP...
PLEASE, WILL YOU LIFT YOUR CURSE?
-CHUCKLE-
MY PRINCESS, I AM SORRY, I DO NOT MEAN TO LAUGH, BUT--
--THERE IS *NO CURSE!*
WHAT?!
WHAT AILED YOU WAS WORKING ALL HOURS IN YOUR LAB AND FAILING TO GIVE YOURSELF A BREAK.
BUT THEN, WHY WOULD YOU SEND ME FOR THESE THINGS?
YOU NEEDED FRESH AIR--AND TO USE YOUR MIND AND BODY FOR SOMETHING *OTHER THAN* WORK.
I KNEW YOU WOULD NOT LISTEN TO ME IF I SAID THAT, SO I FIGURED I WOULD CAPTURE TWO BIRDS WITH ONE NET.
WHAT DO THEY EVEN DO?

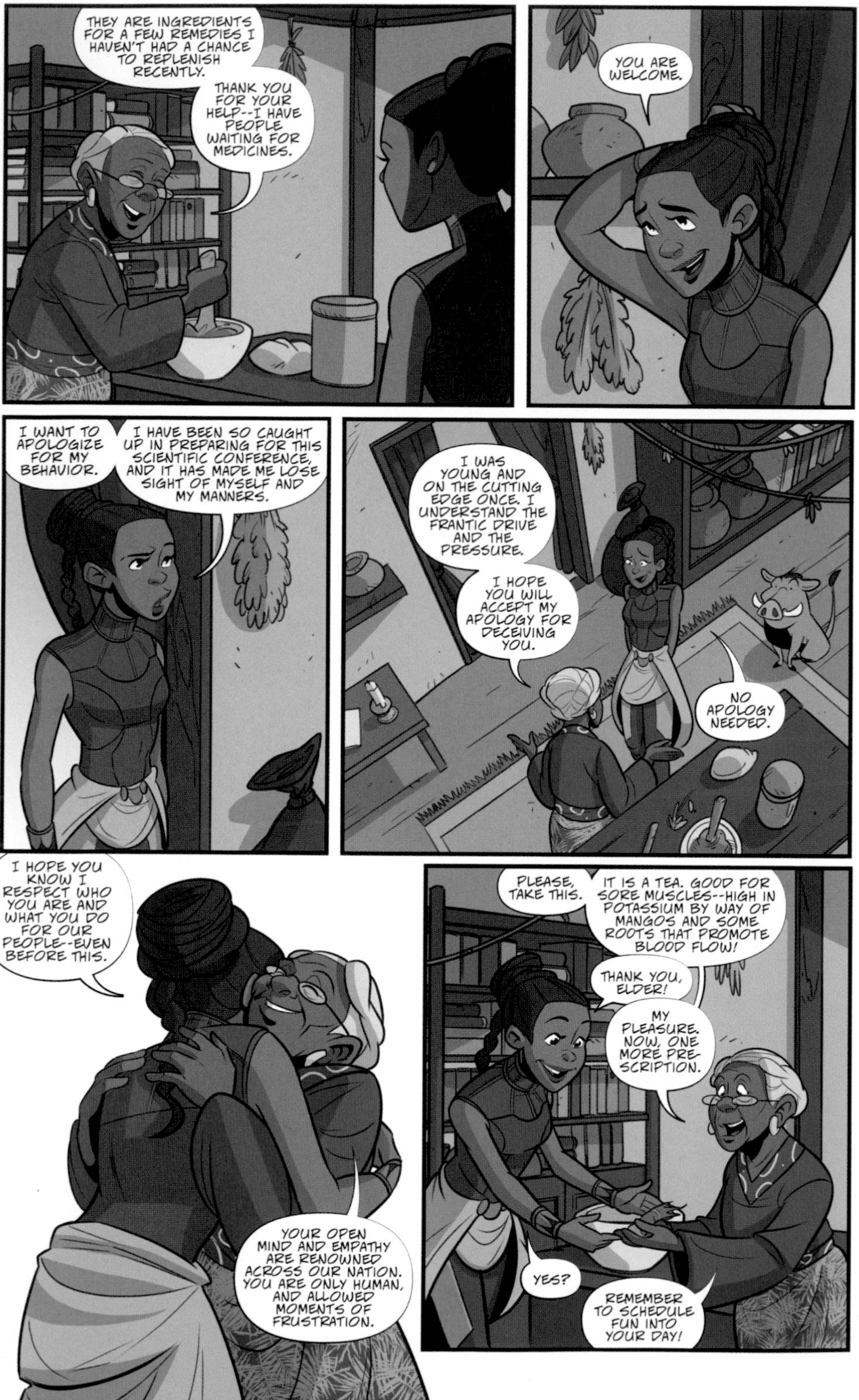
THEY ARE INGREDIENTS FOR A FEW REMEDIES I HAVEN'T HAD A CHANCE TO REPLENISH RECENTLY.
THANK YOU FOR YOUR HELP--I HAVE PEOPLE WAITING FOR MEDICINES.
YOU ARE WELCOME.
I WANT TO APOLOGIZE FOR MY BEHAVIOR.
I HAVE BEEN SO CAUGHT UP IN PREPARING FOR THIS SCIENTIFIC CONFERENCE, AND IT HAS MADE ME LOSE SIGHT OF MYSELF AND MY MANNERS.
I WAS YOUNG AND ON THE CUTTING EDGE ONCE. I UNDERSTAND THE FRANTIC DRIVE AND THE PRESSURE.
I HOPE YOU WILL ACCEPT MY APOLOGY FOR DECEIVING YOU.
NO APOLOGY NEEDED.
I HOPE YOU KNOW I RESPECT WHO YOU ARE AND WHAT YOU DO FOR OUR PEOPLE--EVEN BEFORE THIS.
YOUR OPEN MIND AND EMPATHY ARE RENOWNED ACROSS OUR NATION. YOU ARE ONLY HUMAN, AND ALLOWED MOMENTS OF FRUSTRATION.
PLEASE, TAKE THIS.
IT IS A TEA. GOOD FOR SORE MUSCLES--HIGH IN POTASSIUM BY WAY OF MANGOS AND SOME ROOTS THAT PROMOTE BLOOD FLOW!
THANK YOU, ELDER!
MY PLEASURE. NOW, ONE MORE PRE-SCRIPTION.
YES?
REMEMBER TO SCHEDULE FUN INTO YOUR DAY!

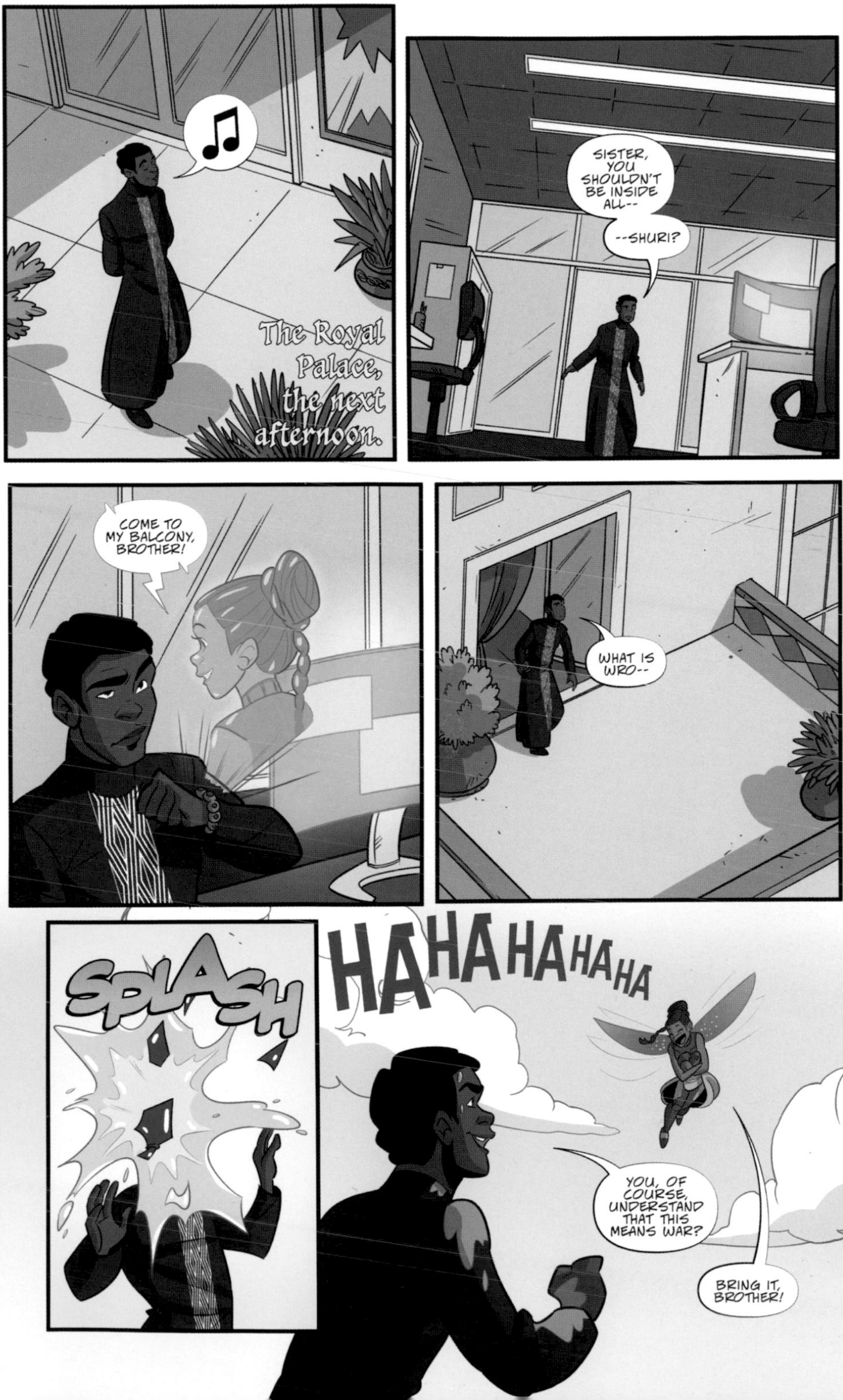
♫
The Royal Palace, the next afternoon.
SISTER, YOU SHOULDN'T BE INSIDE ALL--
--SHURI?
COME TO MY BALCONY, BROTHER!
WHAT IS WRO--
SPLASH
HAHAHAHAHAHA
YOU, OF COURSE, UNDERSTAND THAT THIS MEANS WAR?
BRING IT, BROTHER!

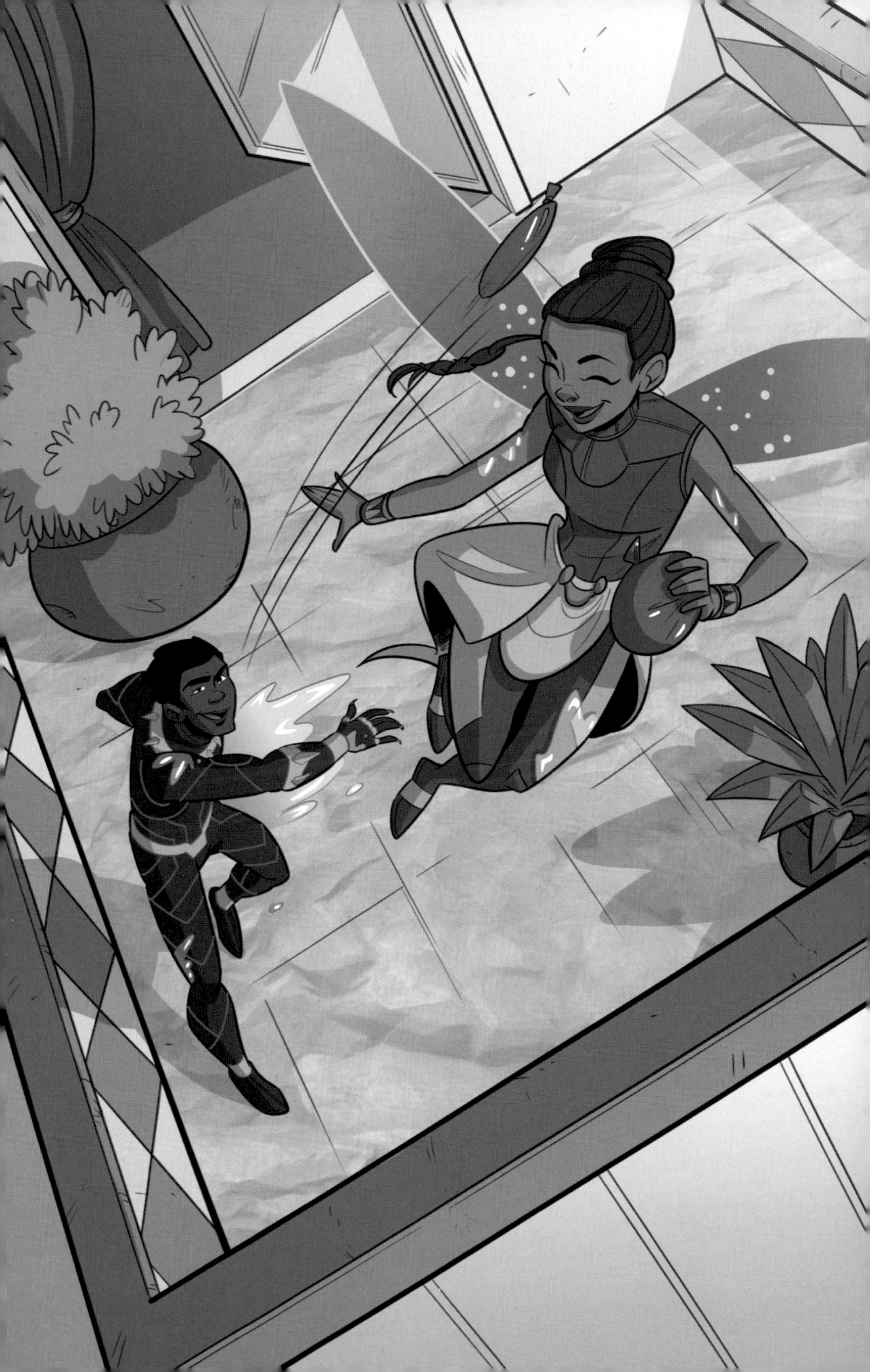

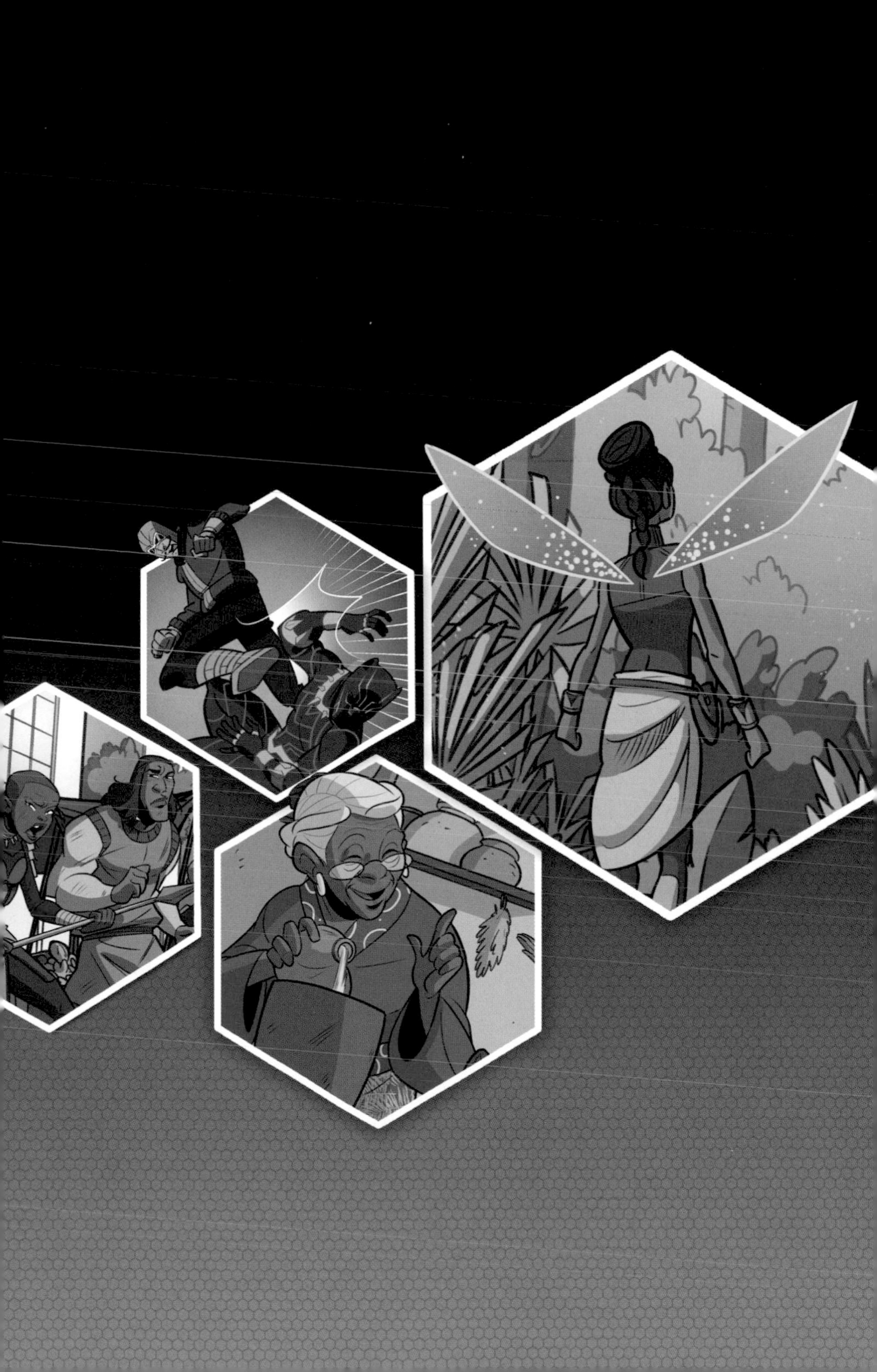

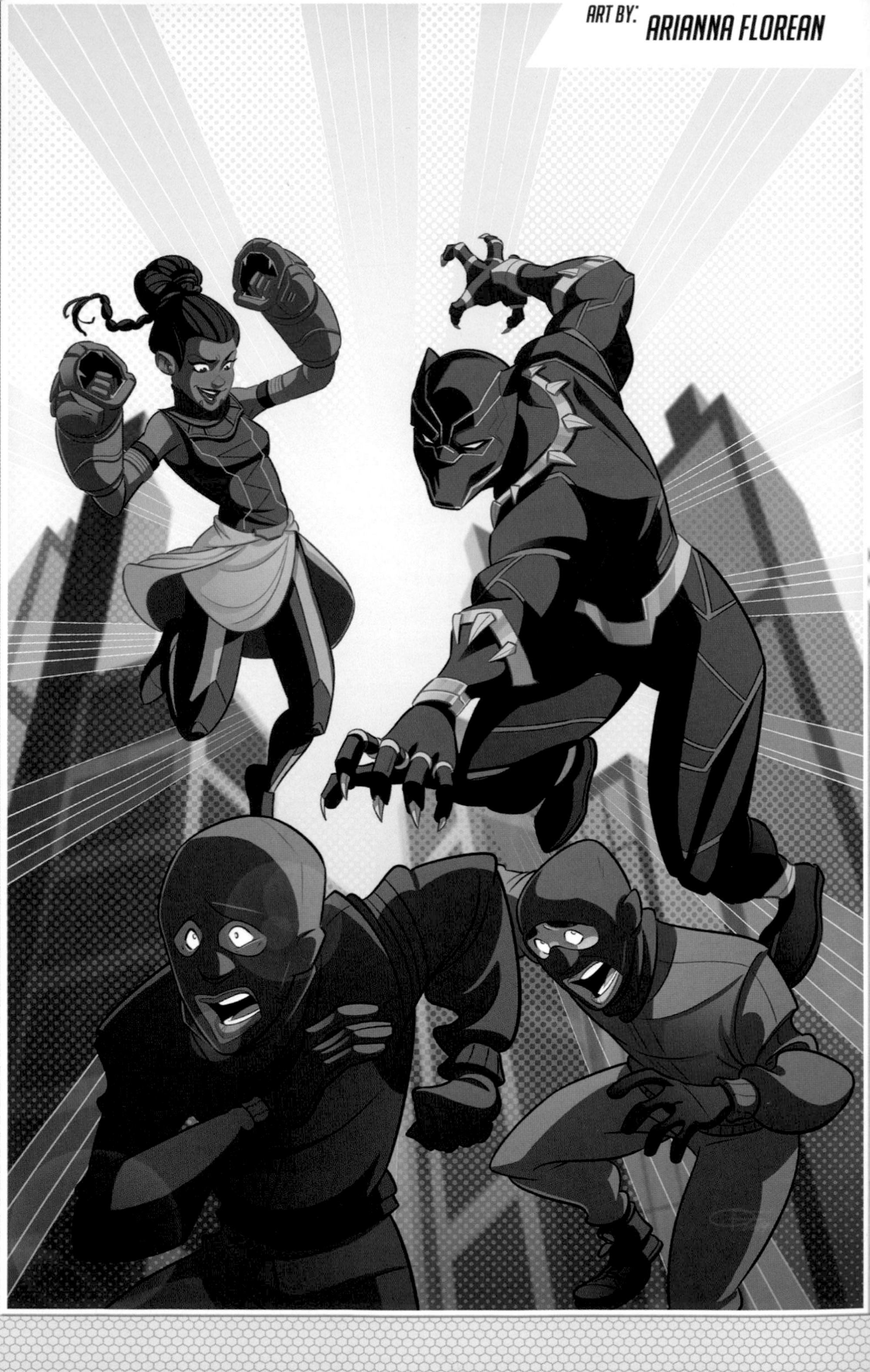
ART BY: ARIANNA FLOREAN

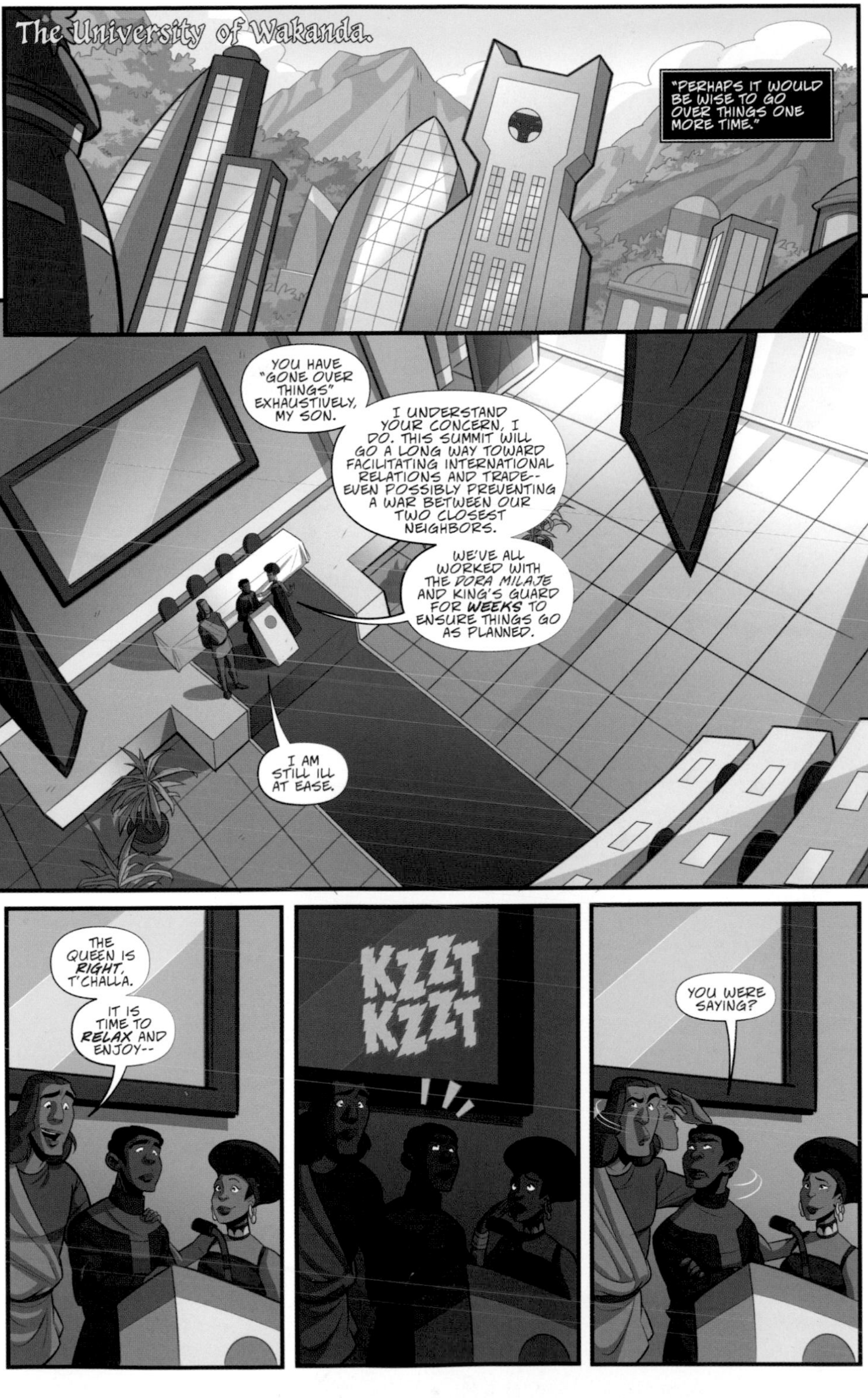
The University of Wakanda.
"PERHAPS IT WOULD BE WISE TO GO OVER THINGS ONE MORE TIME."
YOU HAVE "GONE OVER THINGS" EXHAUSTIVELY, MY SON.
I UNDERSTAND YOUR CONCERN, I DO. THIS SUMMIT WILL GO A LONG WAY TOWARD FACILITATING INTERNATIONAL RELATIONS AND TRADE--EVEN POSSIBLY PREVENTING A WAR BETWEEN OUR TWO CLOSEST NEIGHBORS.
WE'VE ALL WORKED WITH THE DORA MILAJE AND KING'S GUARD FOR WEEKS TO ENSURE THINGS GO AS PLANNED.
I AM STILL ILL AT EASE.
THE QUEEN IS RIGHT, T'CHALLA.
IT IS TIME TO RELAX AND ENJOY--
KZZT KZZT
YOU WERE SAYING?

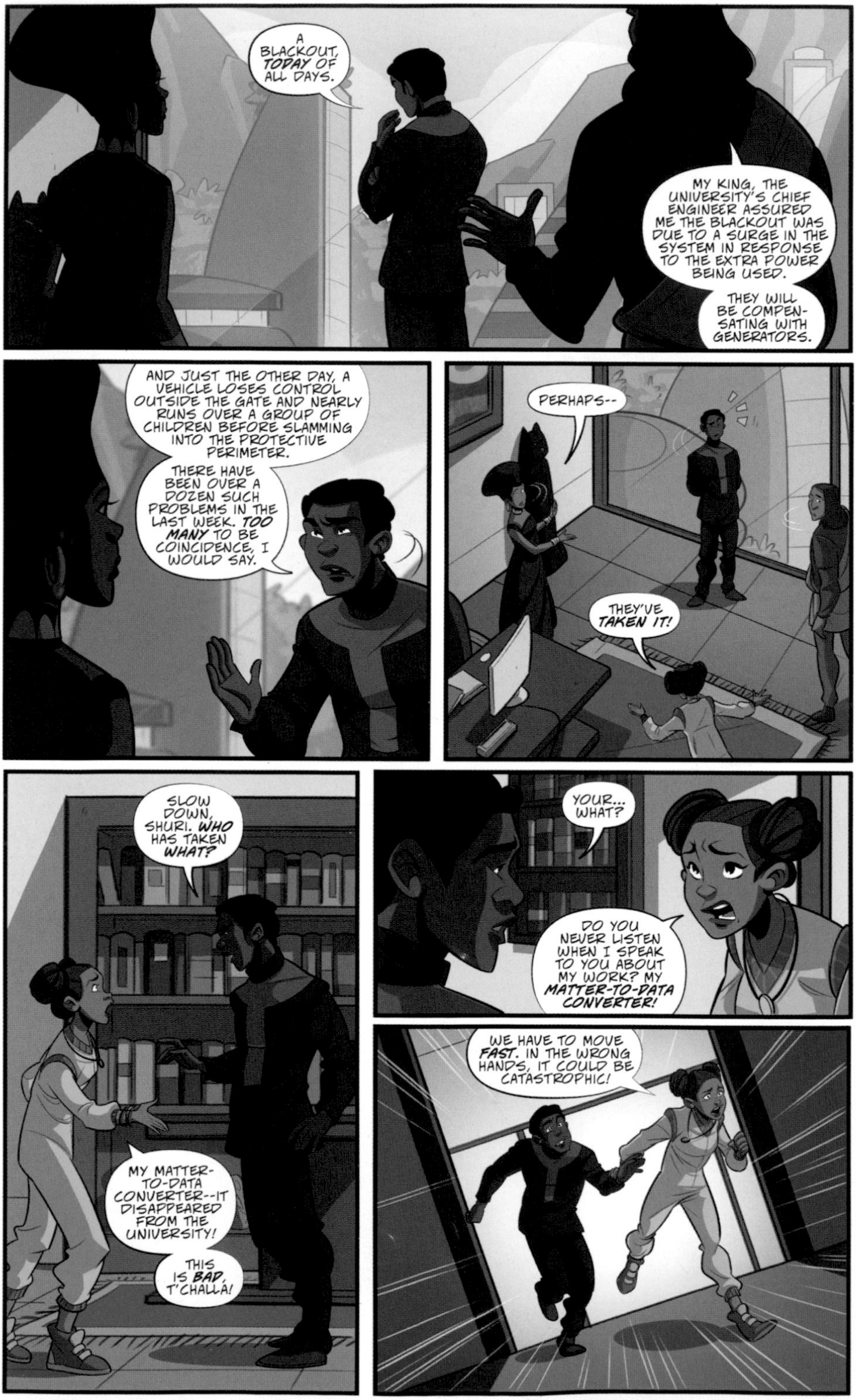
A BLACKOUT, TODAY OF ALL DAYS.
MY KING, THE UNIVERSITY'S CHIEF ENGINEER ASSURED ME THE BLACKOUT WAS DUE TO A SURGE IN THE SYSTEM IN RESPONSE TO THE EXTRA POWER BEING USED.
THEY WILL BE COMPEN-SATING WITH GENERATORS.
AND JUST THE OTHER DAY, A VEHICLE LOSES CONTROL OUTSIDE THE GATE AND NEARLY RUNS OVER A GROUP OF CHILDREN BEFORE SLAMMING INTO THE PROTECTIVE PERIMETER.
THERE HAVE BEEN OVER A DOZEN SUCH PROBLEMS IN THE LAST WEEK. TOO MANY TO BE COINCIDENCE, I WOULD SAY.
PERHAPS--
THEY'VE TAKEN IT!
SLOW DOWN, SHURI. WHO HAS TAKEN WHAT?
MY MATTER-TO-DATA CONVERTER--IT DISAPPEARED FROM THE UNIVERSITY!
THIS IS BAD, T'CHALLA!
YOUR... WHAT?
DO YOU NEVER LISTEN WHEN I SPEAK TO YOU ABOUT MY WORK? MY MATTER-TO-DATA CONVERTER!
WE HAVE TO MOVE FAST. IN THE WRONG HANDS, IT COULD BE CATASTROPHIC!

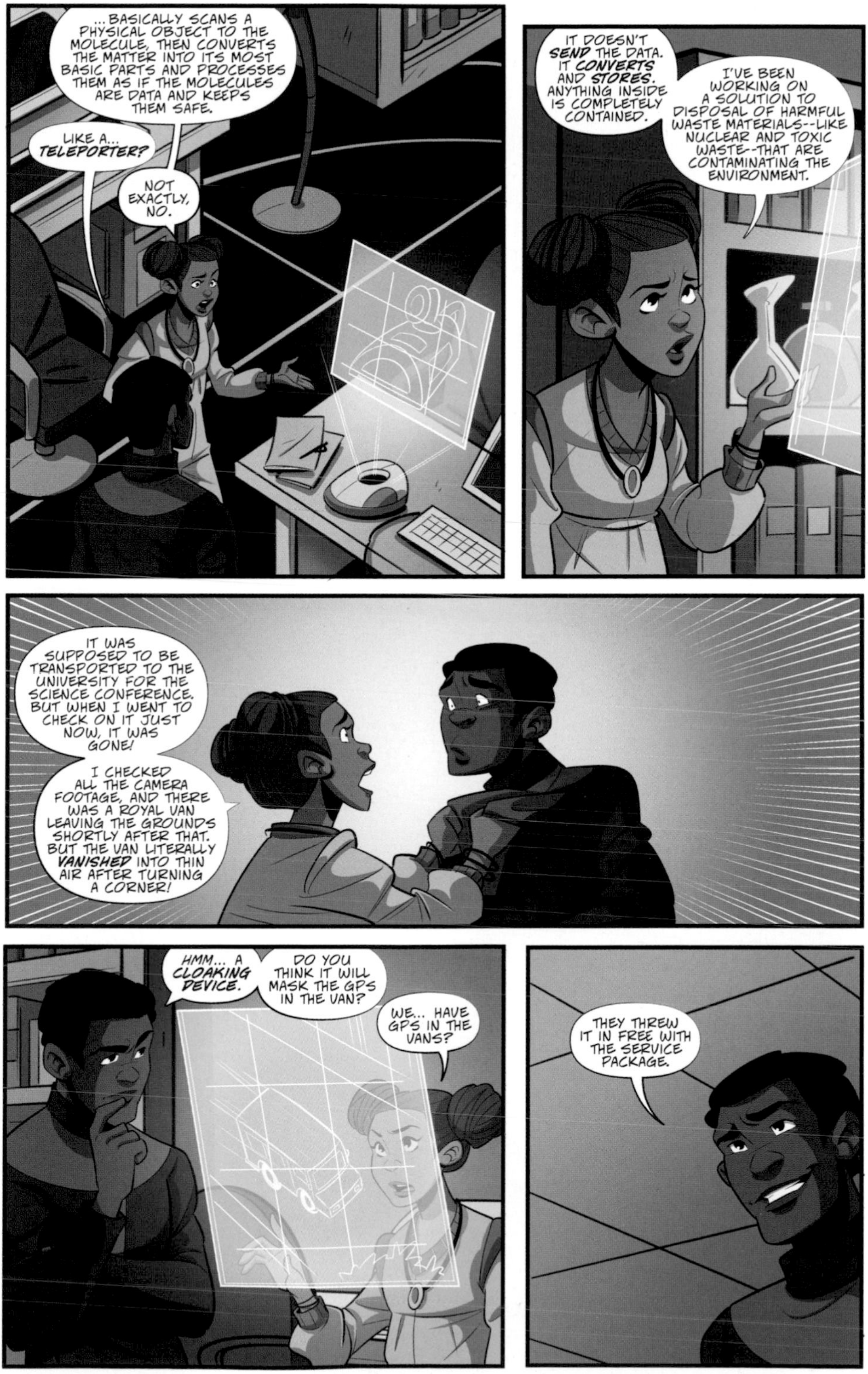
...BASICALLY SCANS A PHYSICAL OBJECT TO THE MOLECULE, THEN CONVERTS THE MATTER INTO ITS MOST BASIC PARTS AND PROCESSES THEM AS IF THE MOLECULES ARE DATA AND KEEPS THEM SAFE.
LIKE A... TELEPORTER?
NOT EXACTLY, NO.
IT DOESN'T SEND THE DATA. IT CONVERTS AND STORES. ANYTHING INSIDE IS COMPLETELY CONTAINED.
I'VE BEEN WORKING ON A SOLUTION TO DISPOSAL OF HARMFUL WASTE MATERIALS--LIKE NUCLEAR AND TOXIC WASTE--THAT ARE CONTAMINATING THE ENVIRONMENT.
IT WAS SUPPOSED TO BE TRANSPORTED TO THE UNIVERSITY FOR THE SCIENCE CONFERENCE. BUT WHEN I WENT TO CHECK ON IT JUST NOW, IT WAS GONE!
I CHECKED ALL THE CAMERA FOOTAGE, AND THERE WAS A ROYAL VAN LEAVING THE GROUNDS SHORTLY AFTER THAT. BUT THE VAN LITERALLY VANISHED INTO THIN AIR AFTER TURNING A CORNER!
HMM... A CLOAKING DEVICE.
DO YOU THINK IT WILL MASK THE GPS IN THE VAN?
WE... HAVE GPS IN THE VANS?
THEY THREW IT IN FREE WITH THE SERVICE PACKAGE.

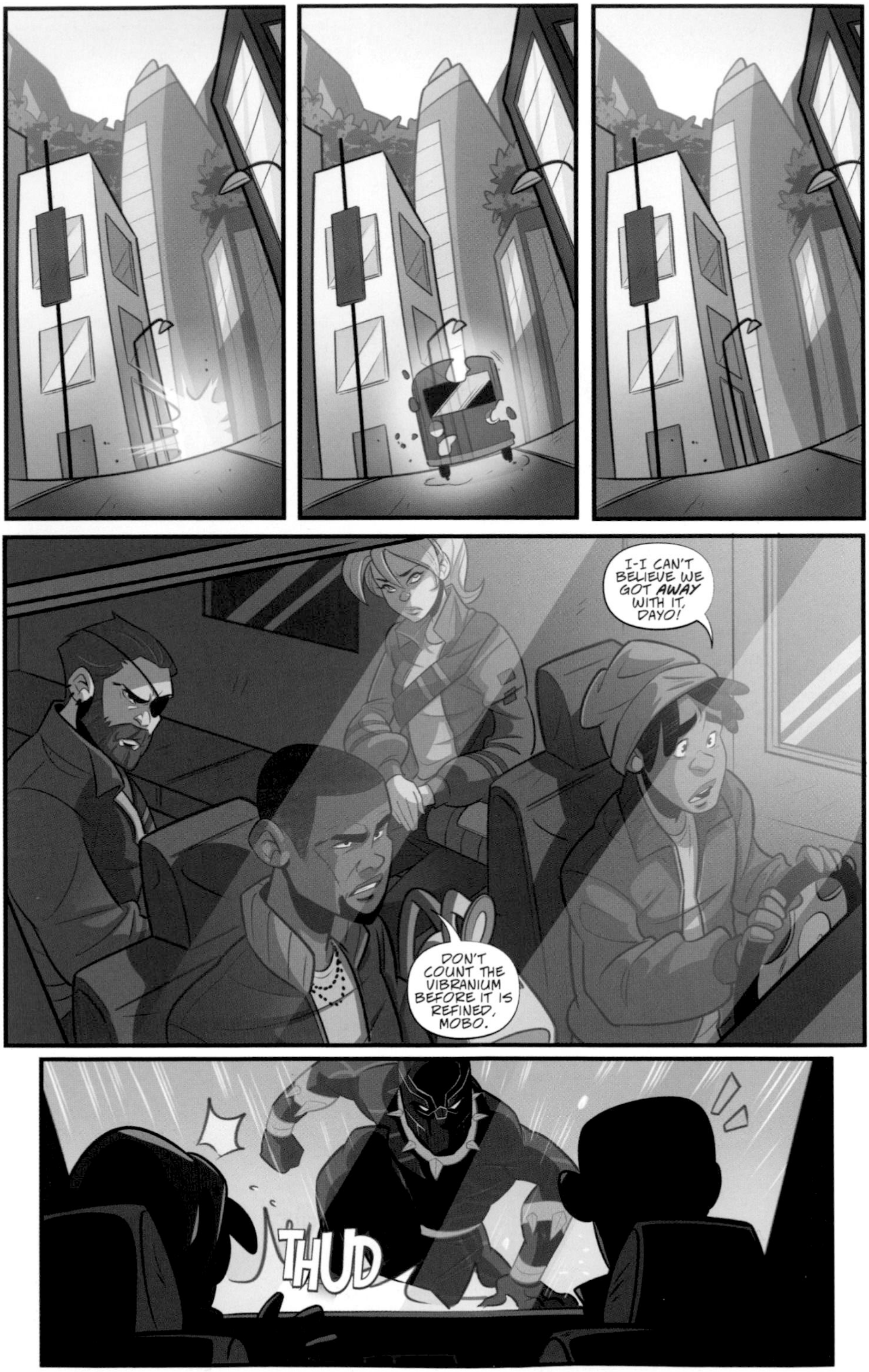
I-I CAN'T BELIEVE WE GOT AWAY WITH IT, DAYO!
DON'T COUNT THE VIBRANIUM BEFORE IT IS REFINED, MOBO.
THUD

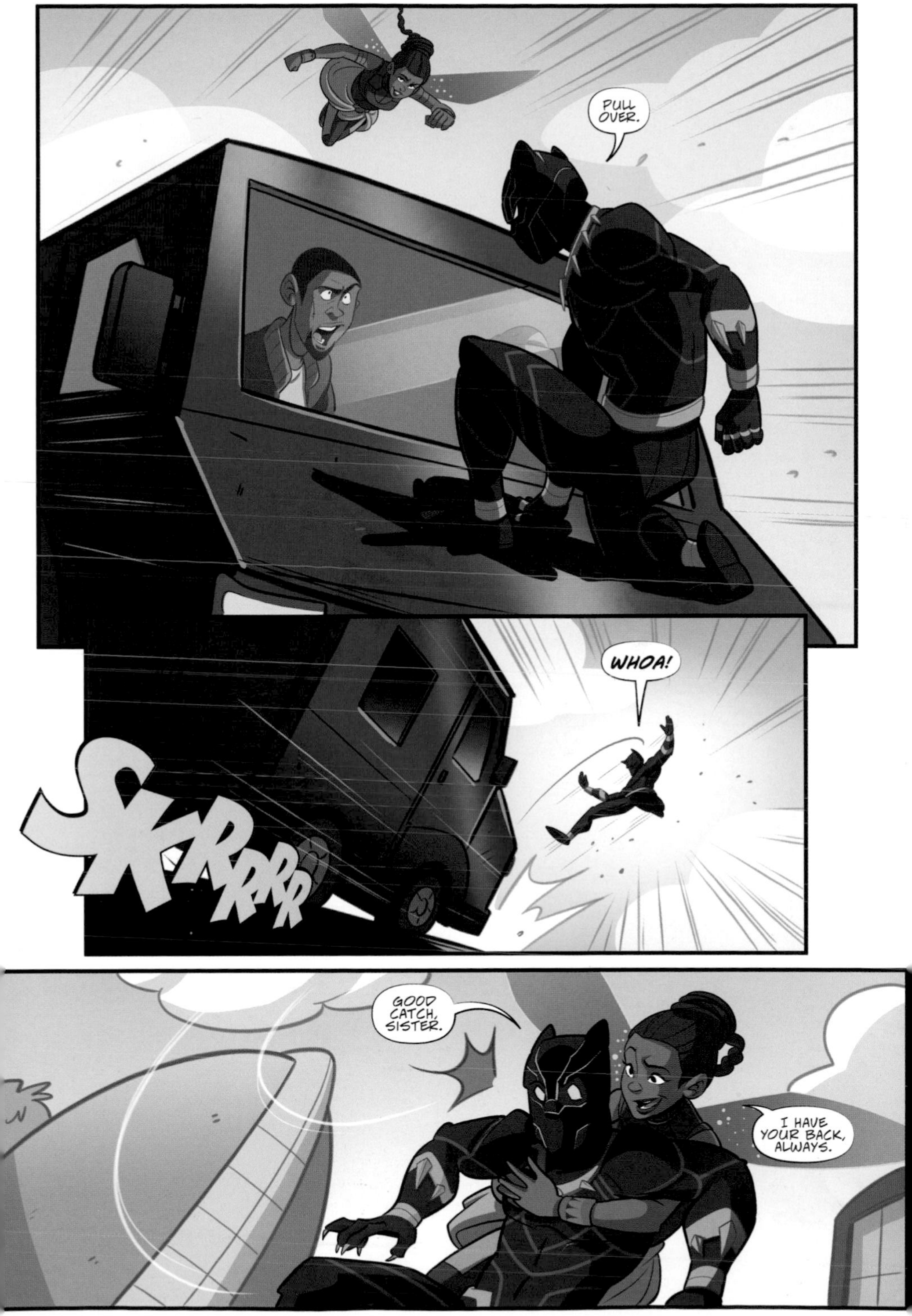
PULL OVER.
WHOA!
SKRRRRR
GOOD CATCH, SISTER.
I HAVE YOUR BACK, ALWAYS.

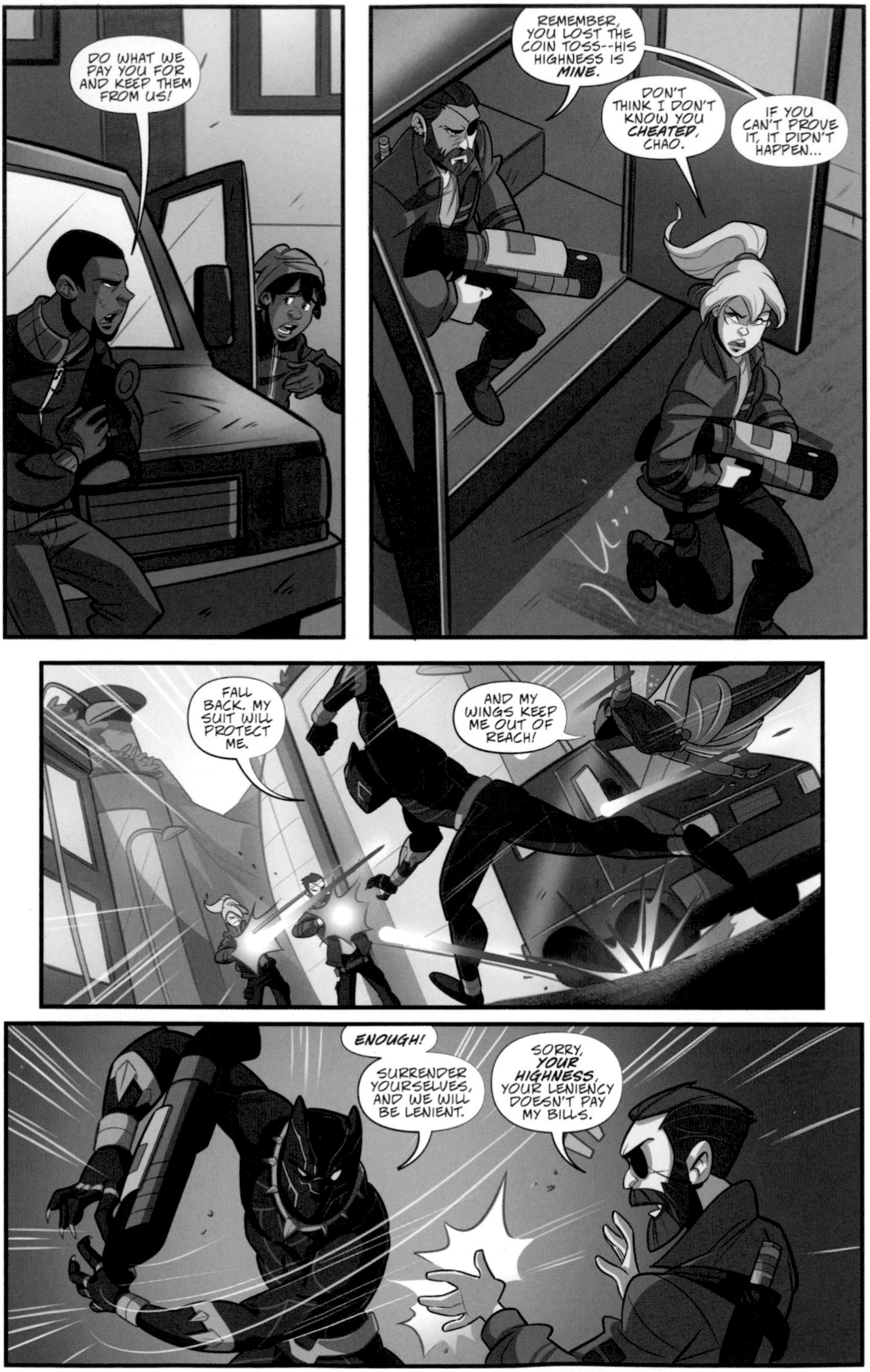
DO WHAT WE PAY YOU FOR AND KEEP THEM FROM US!
REMEMBER, YOU LOST THE COIN TOSS--HIS HIGHNESS IS MINE.
DON'T THINK I DON'T KNOW YOU CHEATED, CHAO.
IF YOU CAN'T PROVE IT, IT DIDN'T HAPPEN...
FALL BACK. MY SUIT WILL PROTECT ME.
AND MY WINGS KEEP ME OUT OF REACH!
ENOUGH!
SURRENDER YOURSELVES, AND WE WILL BE LENIENT.
SORRY, YOUR HIGHNESS, YOUR LENIENCY DOESN'T PAY MY BILLS.

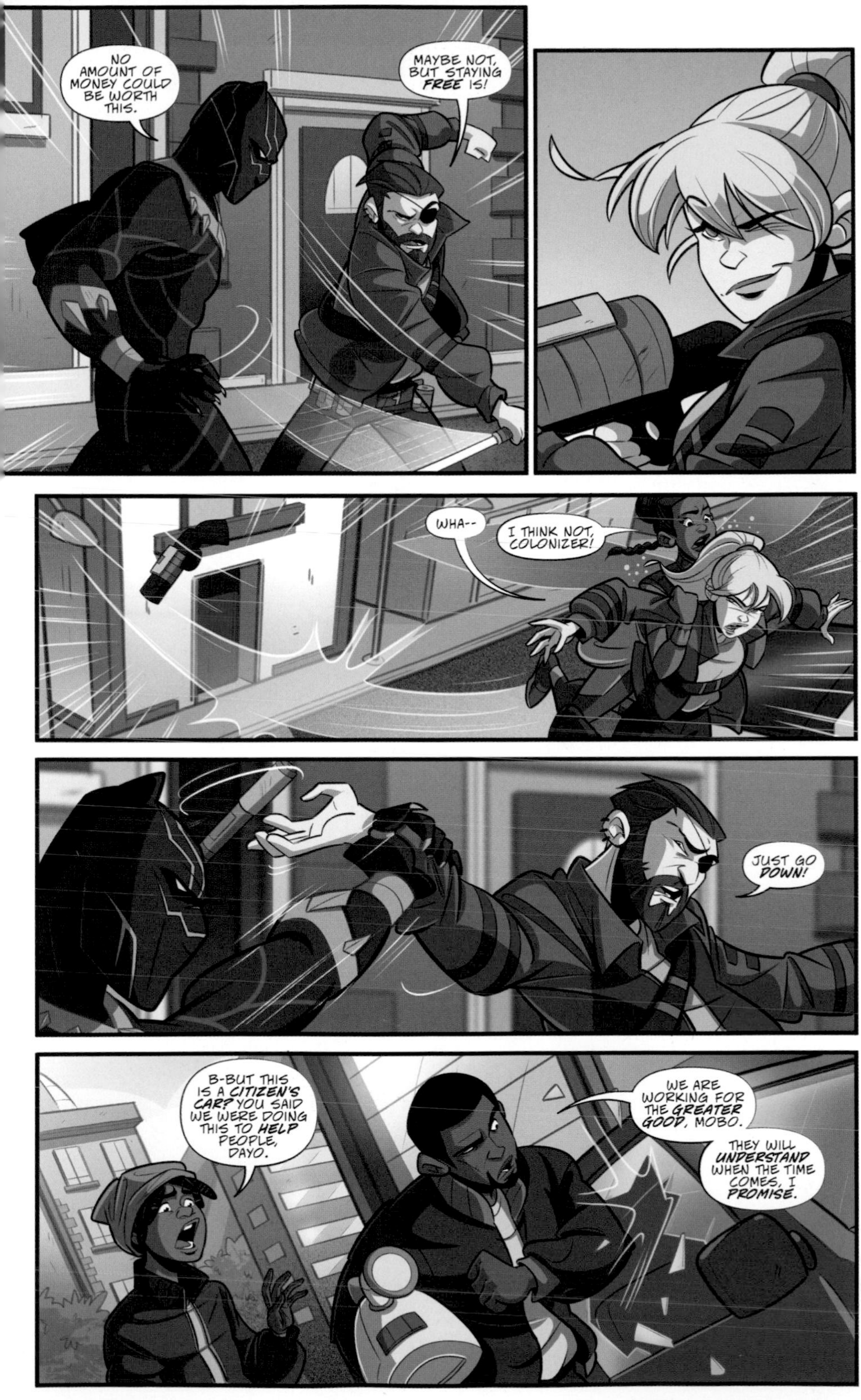
NO AMOUNT OF MONEY COULD BE WORTH THIS.
MAYBE NOT, BUT STAYING FREE IS!
WHA--
I THINK NOT, COLONIZER!
JUST GO DOWN!
B-BUT THIS IS A CITIZEN'S CAR? YOU SAID WE WERE DOING THIS TO HELP PEOPLE, DAYO.
WE ARE WORKING FOR THE GREATER GOOD, MOBO.
THEY WILL UNDERSTAND WHEN THE TIME COMES, I PROMISE.

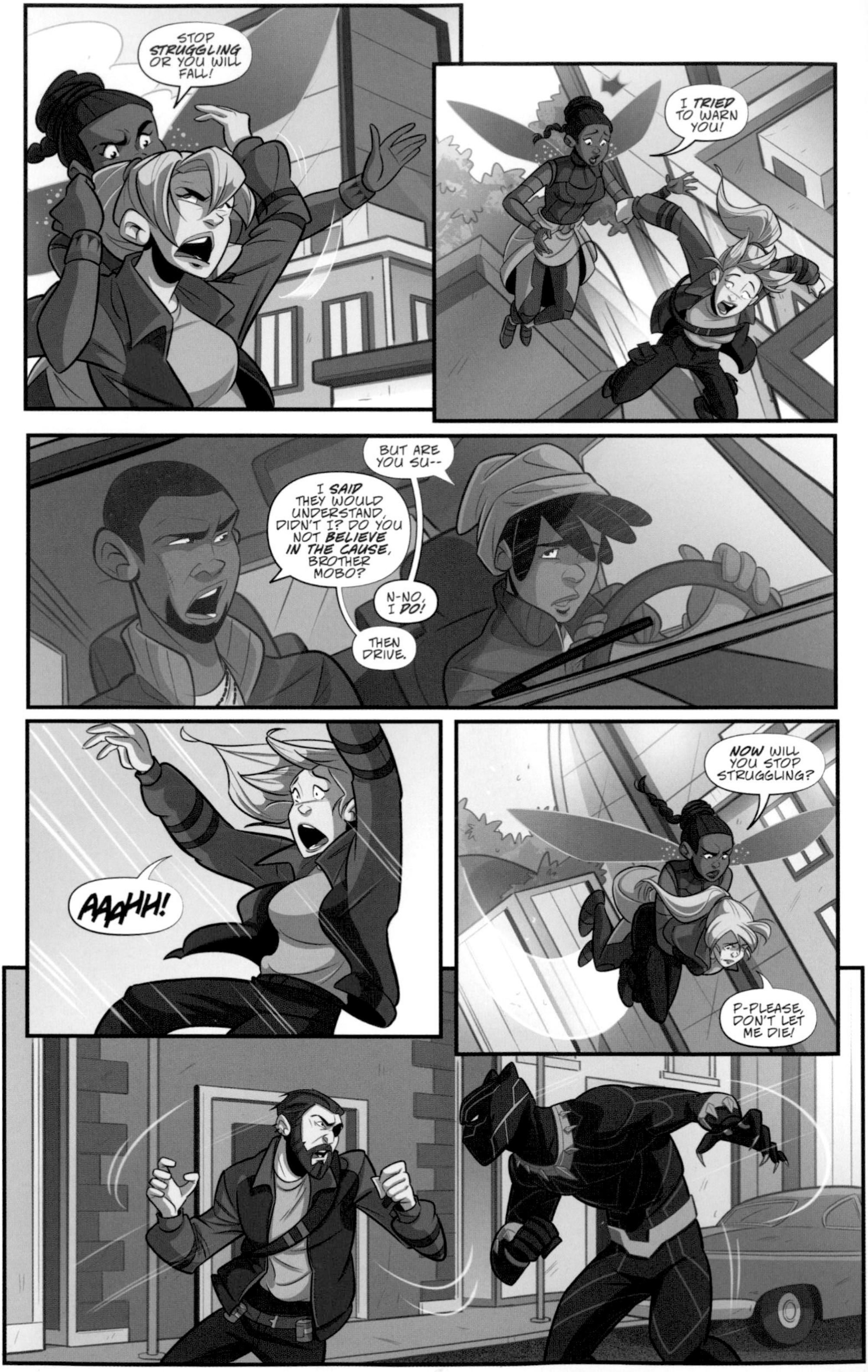
STOP STRUGGLING OR YOU WILL FALL!
I TRIED TO WARN YOU!
BUT ARE YOU SU--
I SAID THEY WOULD UNDERSTAND, DIDN'T I? DO YOU NOT BELIEVE IN THE CAUSE, BROTHER MOBO?
N-NO, I DO!
THEN DRIVE.
AAAHH!
NOW WILL YOU STOP STRUGGLING?
P-PLEASE, DON'T LET ME DIE!

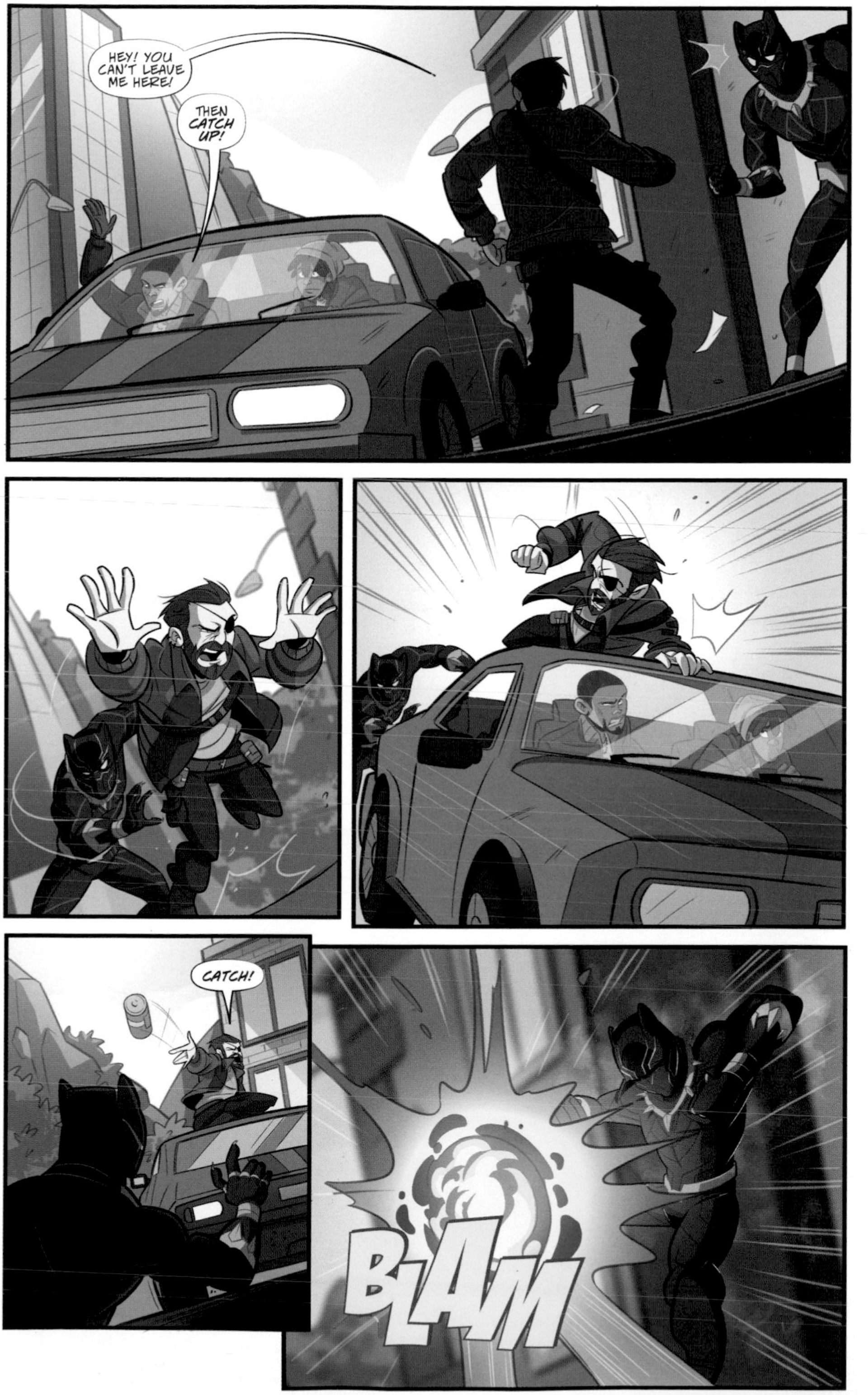
HEY! YOU CAN'T LEAVE ME HERE!
THEN CATCH UP!
CATCH!
BLAM

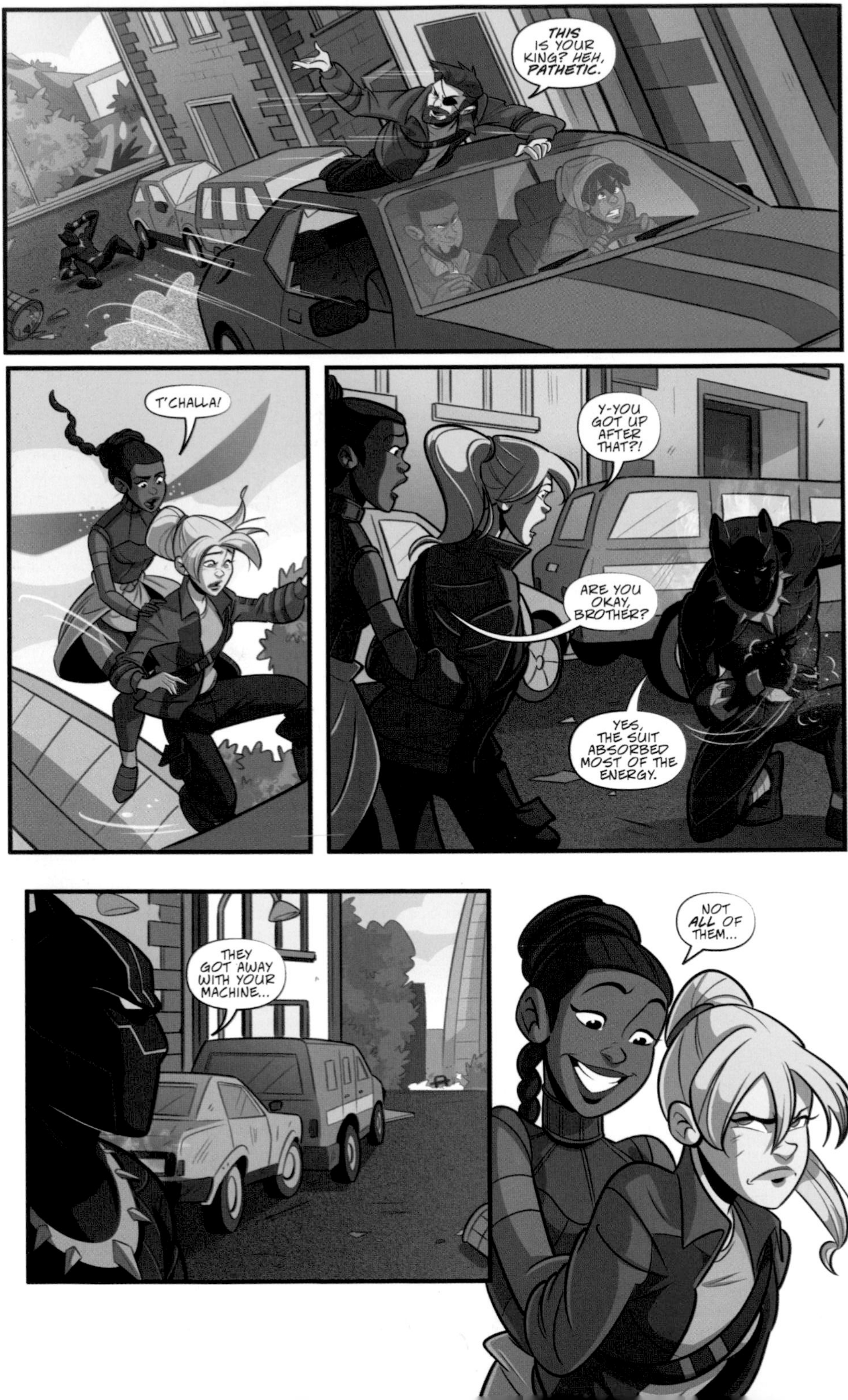
THIS IS YOUR KING? HEH, PATHETIC.
T'CHALLA!
Y-YOU GOT UP AFTER THAT?!
ARE YOU OKAY, BROTHER?
YES, THE SUIT ABSORBED MOST OF THE ENERGY.
THEY GOT AWAY WITH YOUR MACHINE...
NOT ALL OF THEM...

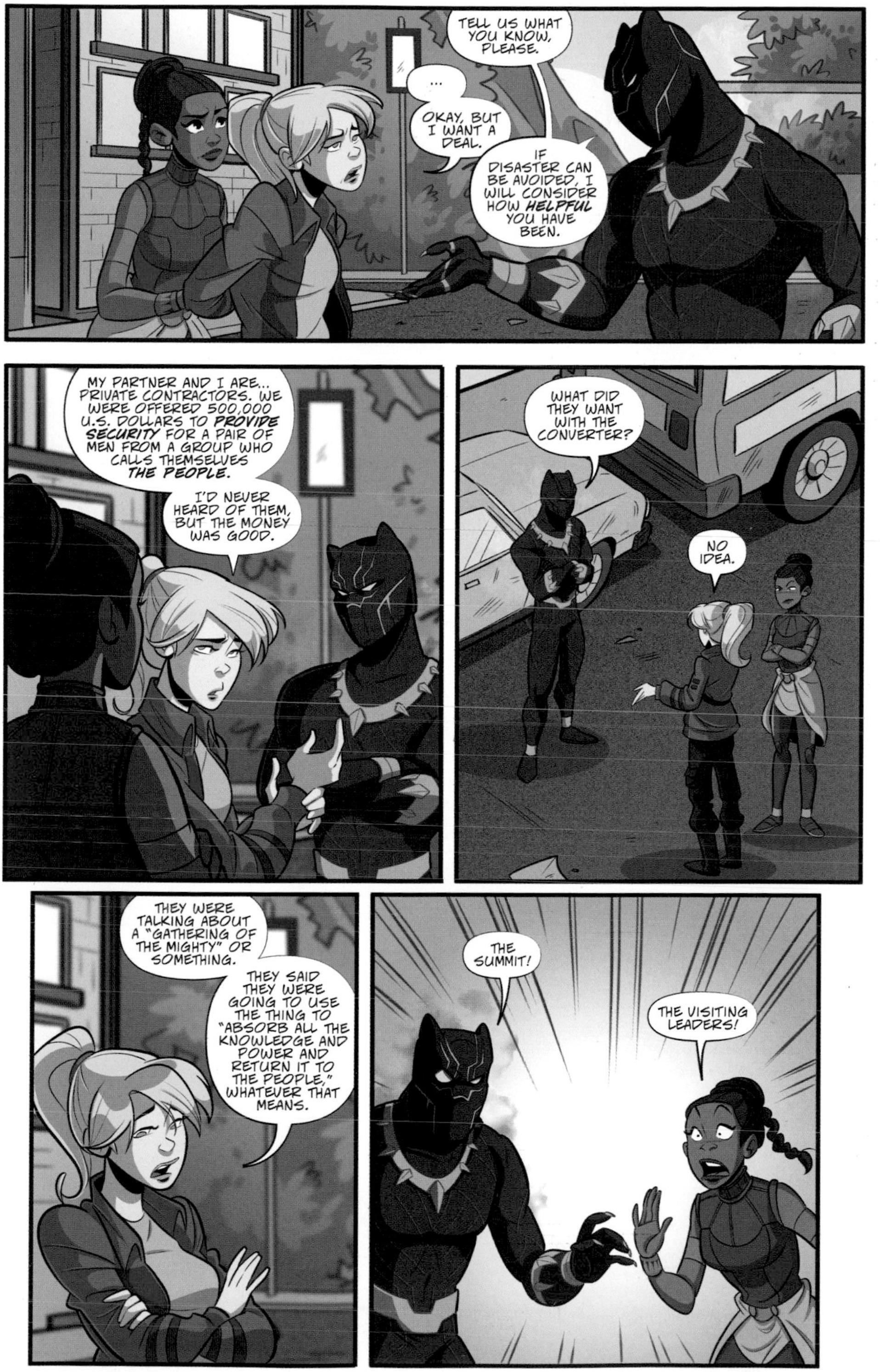
TELL US WHAT YOU KNOW, PLEASE.
...
OKAY, BUT I WANT A DEAL.
IF DISASTER CAN BE AVOIDED, I WILL CONSIDER HOW HELPFUL YOU HAVE BEEN.
MY PARTNER AND I ARE... PRIVATE CONTRACTORS. WE WERE OFFERED 500,000 U.S. DOLLARS TO PROVIDE SECURITY FOR A PAIR OF MEN FROM A GROUP WHO CALLS THEMSELVES THE PEOPLE.
I'D NEVER HEARD OF THEM, BUT THE MONEY WAS GOOD.
WHAT DID THEY WANT WITH THE CONVERTER?
NO IDEA.
THEY WERE TALKING ABOUT A "GATHERING OF THE MIGHTY" OR SOMETHING.
THEY SAID THEY WERE GOING TO USE THE THING TO "ABSORB ALL THE KNOWLEDGE AND POWER AND RETURN IT TO THE PEOPLE," WHATEVER THAT MEANS.
THE SUMMIT!
THE VISITING LEADERS!

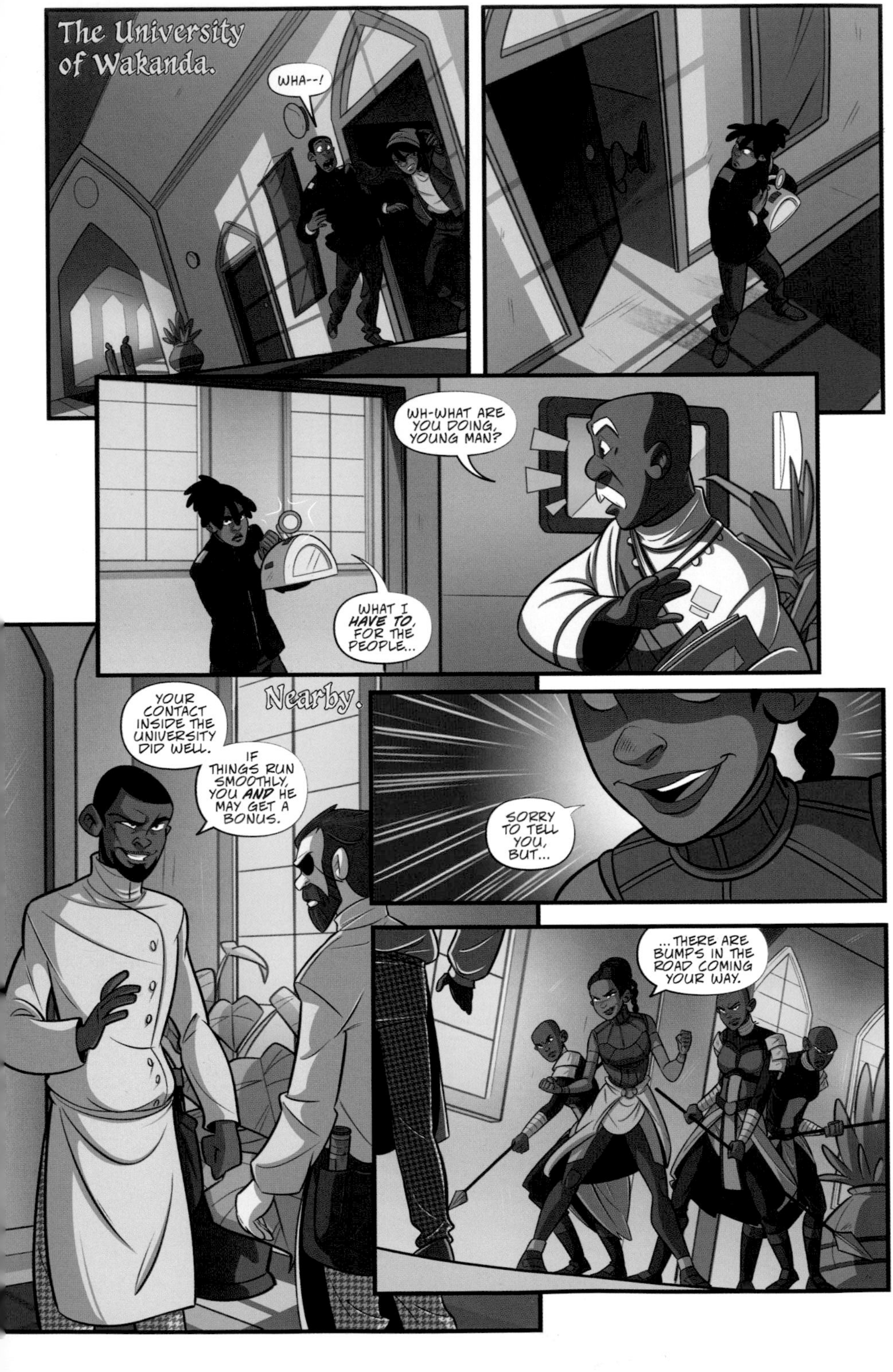

The University of Wakanda.
WHA--!
WH-WHAT ARE YOU DOING, YOUNG MAN?
WHAT I HAVE TO, FOR THE PEOPLE...
Nearby.
YOUR CONTACT INSIDE THE UNIVERSITY DID WELL.
IF THINGS RUN SMOOTHLY, YOU AND HE MAY GET A BONUS.
SORRY TO TELL YOU, BUT...
...THERE ARE BUMPS IN THE ROAD COMING YOUR WAY.

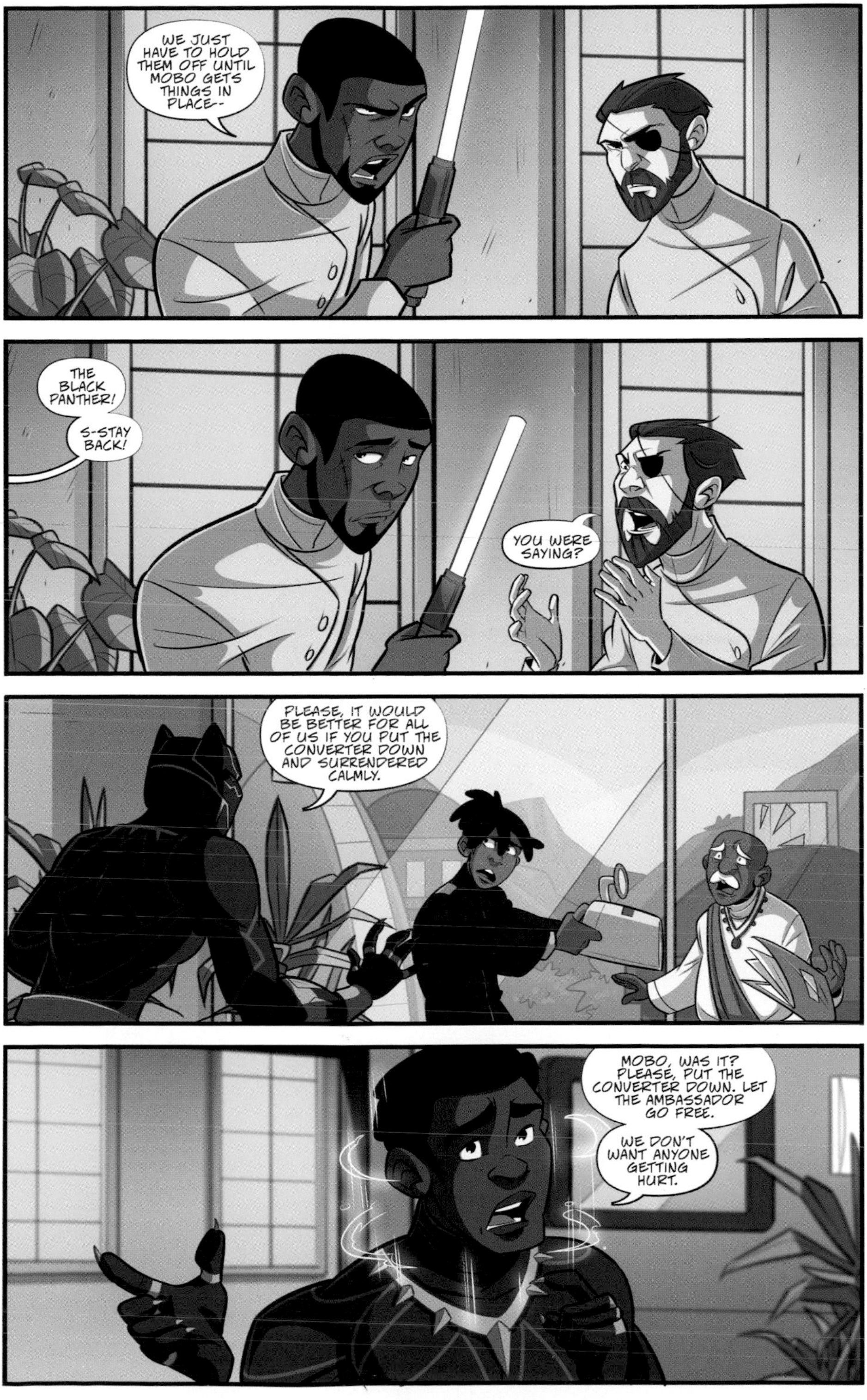
WE JUST HAVE TO HOLD THEM OFF UNTIL MOBO GETS THINGS IN PLACE--
THE BLACK PANTHER!
S-STAY BACK!
YOU WERE SAYING?
PLEASE, IT WOULD BE BETTER FOR ALL OF US IF YOU PUT THE CONVERTER DOWN AND SURRENDERED CALMLY.
MOBO, WAS IT? PLEASE, PUT THE CONVERTER DOWN. LET THE AMBASSADOR GO FREE.
WE DON'T WANT ANYONE GETTING HURT.

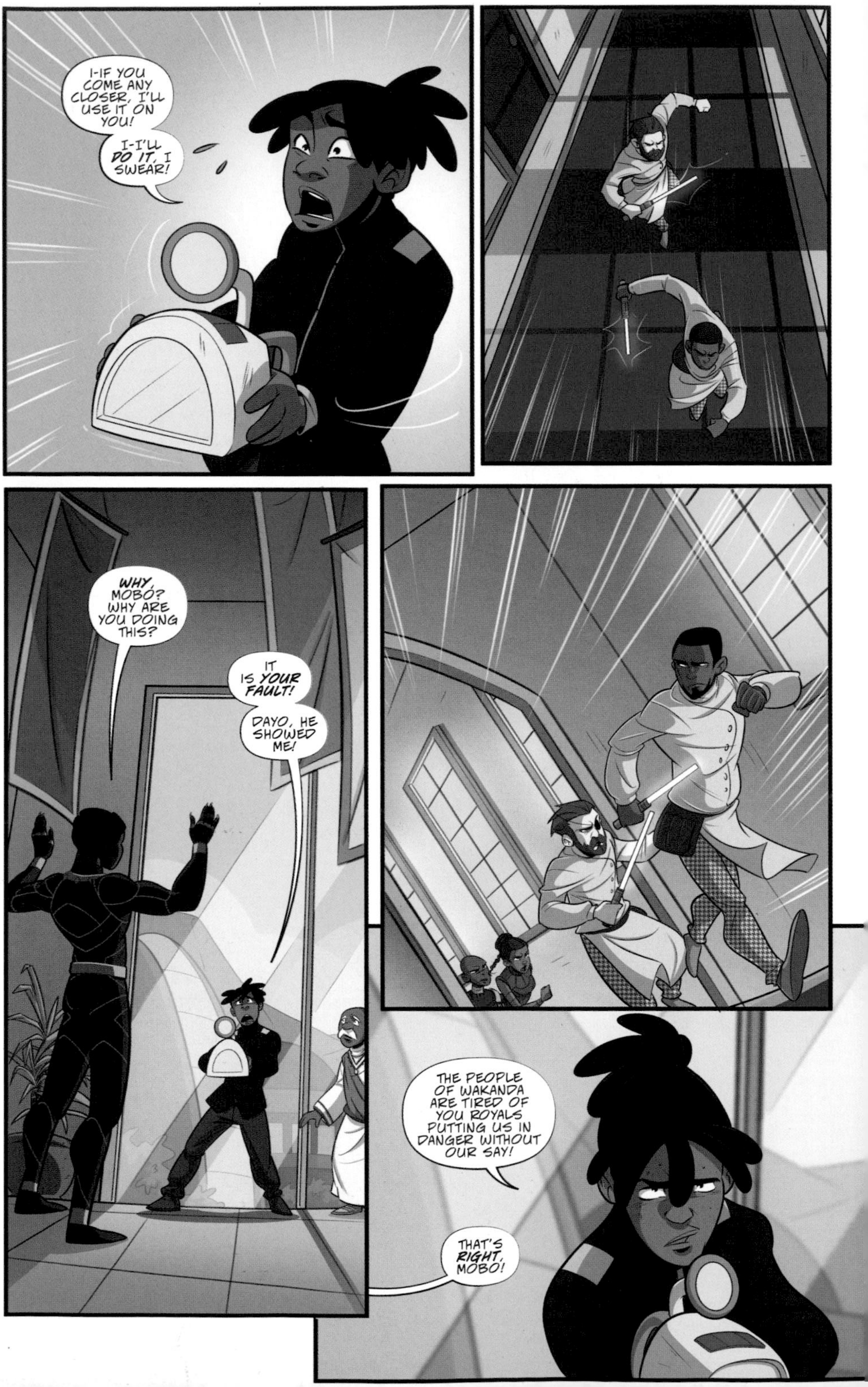
I-IF YOU COME ANY CLOSER, I'LL USE IT ON YOU!
I-I'LL *DO IT*, I SWEAR!
WHY, MOBO? WHY ARE YOU DOING THIS?
IT IS *YOUR FAULT!*
DAYO, HE SHOWED ME!
THE PEOPLE OF WAKANDA ARE TIRED OF YOU ROYALS PUTTING US IN DANGER WITHOUT OUR SAY!
THAT'S *RIGHT*, MOBO!

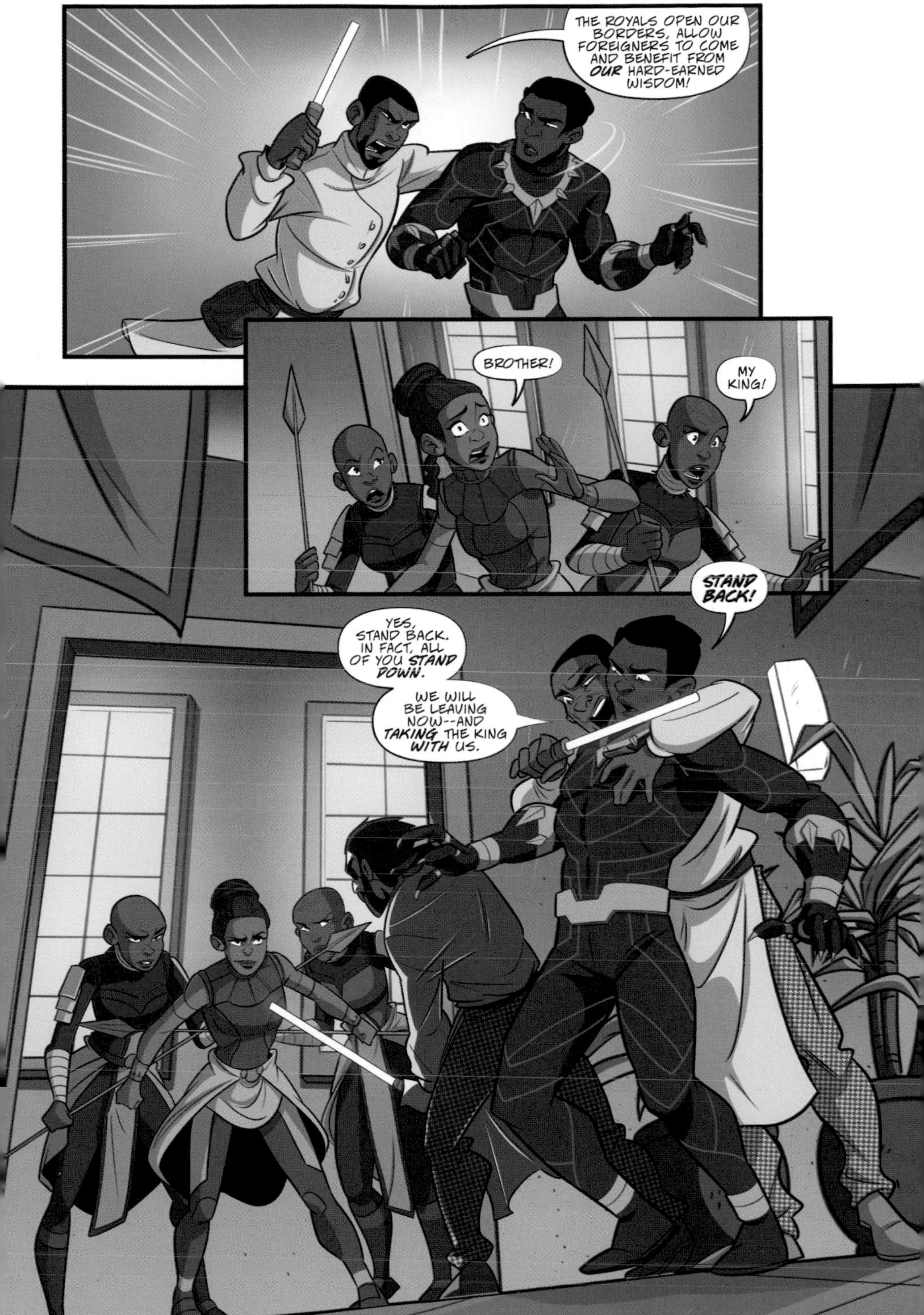
THE ROYALS OPEN OUR BORDERS, ALLOW FOREIGNERS TO COME AND BENEFIT FROM OUR HARD-EARNED WISDOM!
BROTHER!
MY KING!
STAND BACK!
YES, STAND BACK. IN FACT, ALL OF YOU STAND DOWN.
WE WILL BE LEAVING NOW--AND TAKING THE KING WITH US.

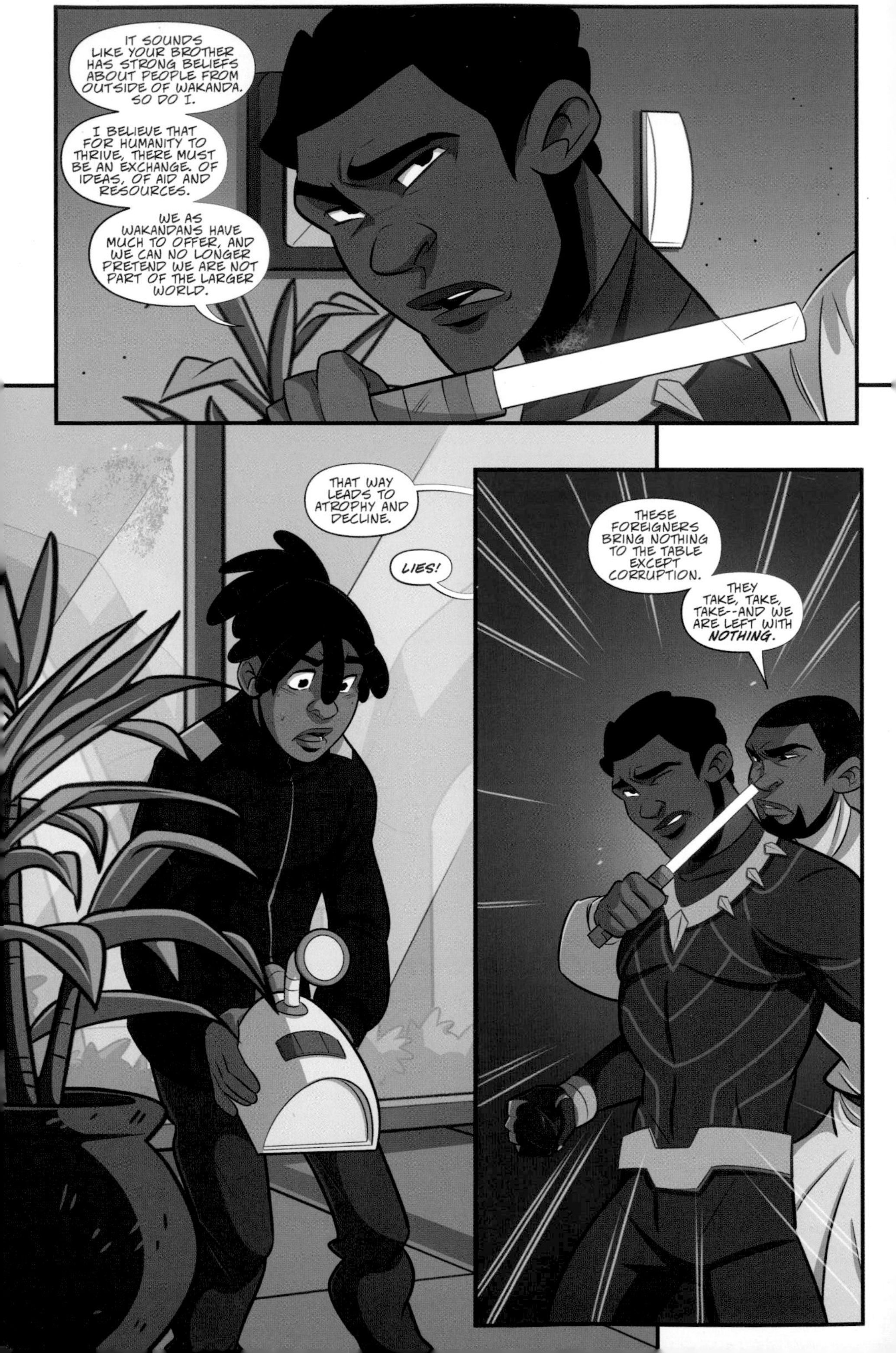
IT SOUNDS LIKE YOUR BROTHER HAS STRONG BELIEFS ABOUT PEOPLE FROM OUTSIDE OF WAKANDA. SO DO I.
I BELIEVE THAT FOR HUMANITY TO THRIVE, THERE MUST BE AN EXCHANGE. OF IDEAS, OF AID AND RESOURCES.
WE AS WAKANDANS HAVE MUCH TO OFFER, AND WE CAN NO LONGER PRETEND WE ARE NOT PART OF THE LARGER WORLD.
THAT WAY LEADS TO ATROPHY AND DECLINE.
LIES!
THESE FOREIGNERS BRING NOTHING TO THE TABLE EXCEPT CORRUPTION.
THEY TAKE, TAKE, TAKE--AND WE ARE LEFT WITH NOTHING.

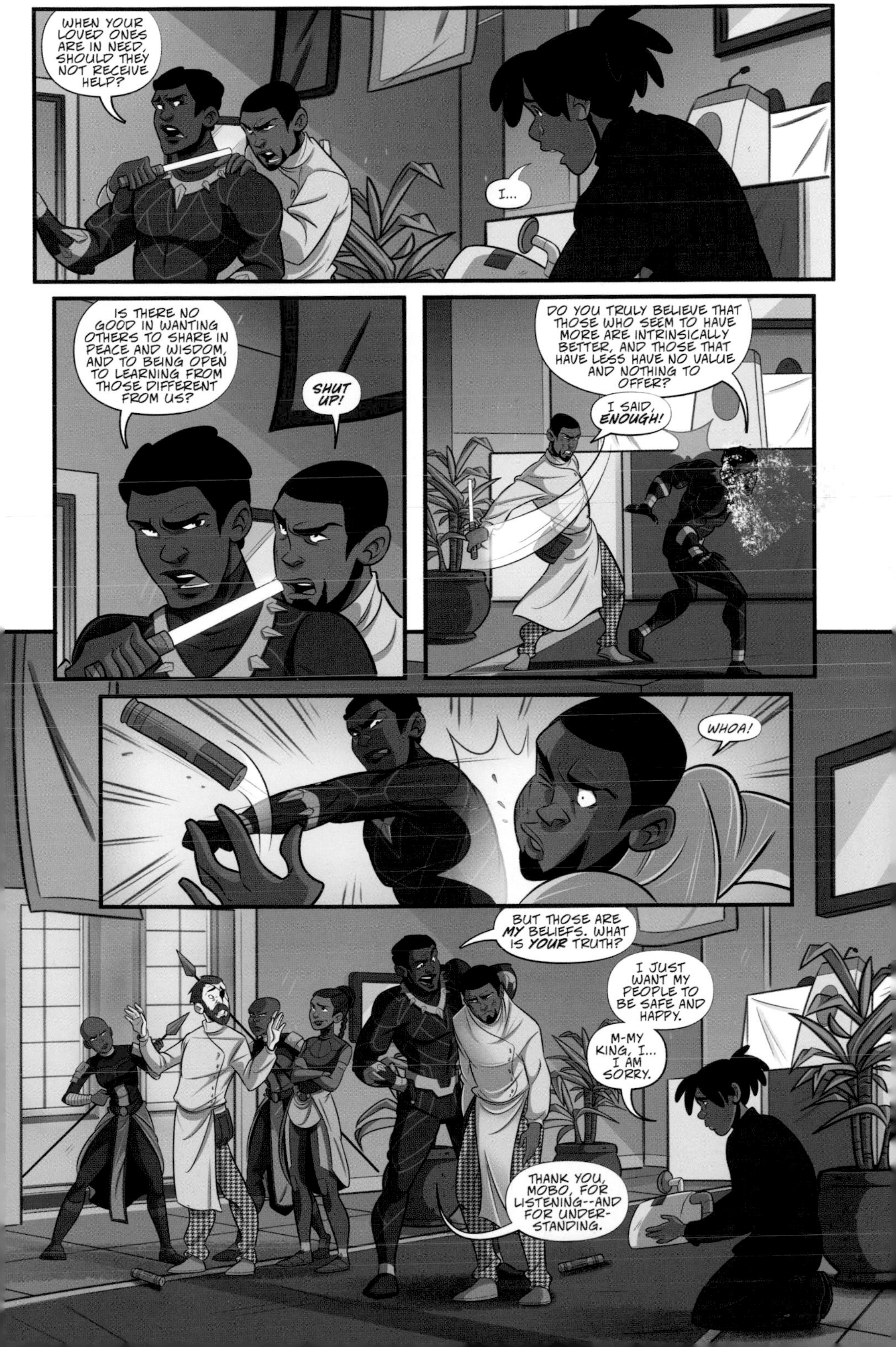
WHEN YOUR LOVED ONES ARE IN NEED, SHOULD THEY NOT RECEIVE HELP?
I...
IS THERE NO GOOD IN WANTING OTHERS TO SHARE IN PEACE AND WISDOM, AND TO BEING OPEN TO LEARNING FROM THOSE DIFFERENT FROM US?
SHUT UP!
DO YOU TRULY BELIEVE THAT THOSE WHO SEEM TO HAVE MORE ARE INTRINSICALLY BETTER, AND THOSE THAT HAVE LESS HAVE NO VALUE AND NOTHING TO OFFER?
I SAID, ENOUGH!
WHOA!
BUT THOSE ARE MY BELIEFS. WHAT IS YOUR TRUTH?
I JUST WANT MY PEOPLE TO BE SAFE AND HAPPY.
M-MY KING, I... I AM SORRY.
THANK YOU, MOBO, FOR LISTENING--AND FOR UNDER-STANDING.

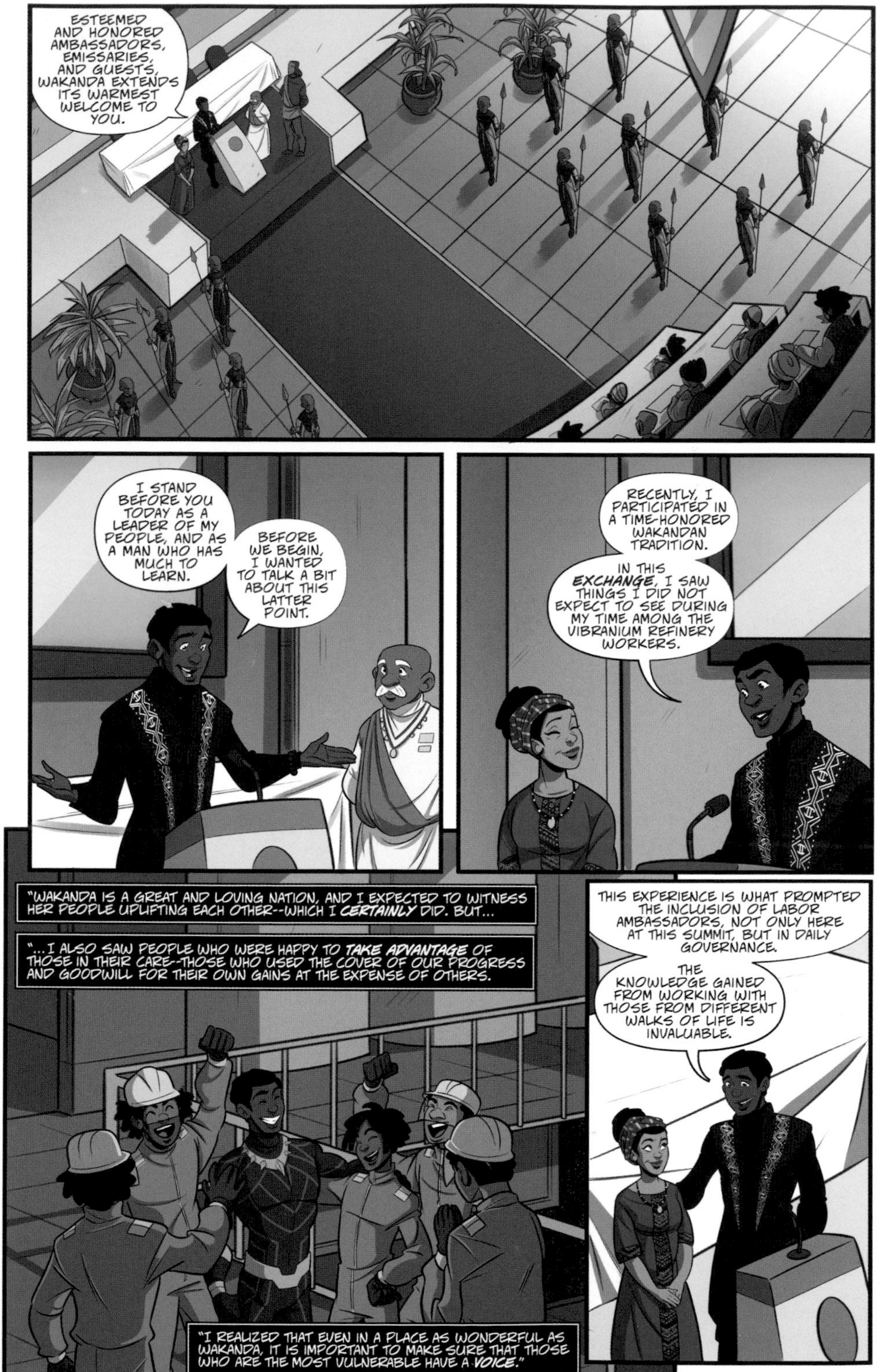
ESTEEMED AND HONORED AMBASSADORS, EMISSARIES, AND GUESTS, WAKANDA EXTENDS ITS WARMEST WELCOME TO YOU.
I STAND BEFORE YOU TODAY AS A LEADER OF MY PEOPLE, AND AS A MAN WHO HAS MUCH TO LEARN.
BEFORE WE BEGIN, I WANTED TO TALK A BIT ABOUT THIS LATTER POINT.
RECENTLY, I PARTICIPATED IN A TIME-HONORED WAKANDAN TRADITION.
IN THIS EXCHANGE, I SAW THINGS I DID NOT EXPECT TO SEE DURING MY TIME AMONG THE VIBRANIUM REFINERY WORKERS.
"WAKANDA IS A GREAT AND LOVING NATION, AND I EXPECTED TO WITNESS HER PEOPLE UPLIFTING EACH OTHER--WHICH I CERTAINLY DID. BUT...
"...I ALSO SAW PEOPLE WHO WERE HAPPY TO TAKE ADVANTAGE OF THOSE IN THEIR CARE--THOSE WHO USED THE COVER OF OUR PROGRESS AND GOODWILL FOR THEIR OWN GAINS AT THE EXPENSE OF OTHERS.
"I REALIZED THAT EVEN IN A PLACE AS WONDERFUL AS WAKANDA, IT IS IMPORTANT TO MAKE SURE THAT THOSE WHO ARE THE MOST VULNERABLE HAVE A VOICE."
THIS EXPERIENCE IS WHAT PROMPTED THE INCLUSION OF LABOR AMBASSADORS, NOT ONLY HERE AT THIS SUMMIT, BUT IN DAILY GOVERNANCE.
THE KNOWLEDGE GAINED FROM WORKING WITH THOSE FROM DIFFERENT WALKS OF LIFE IS INVALUABLE.

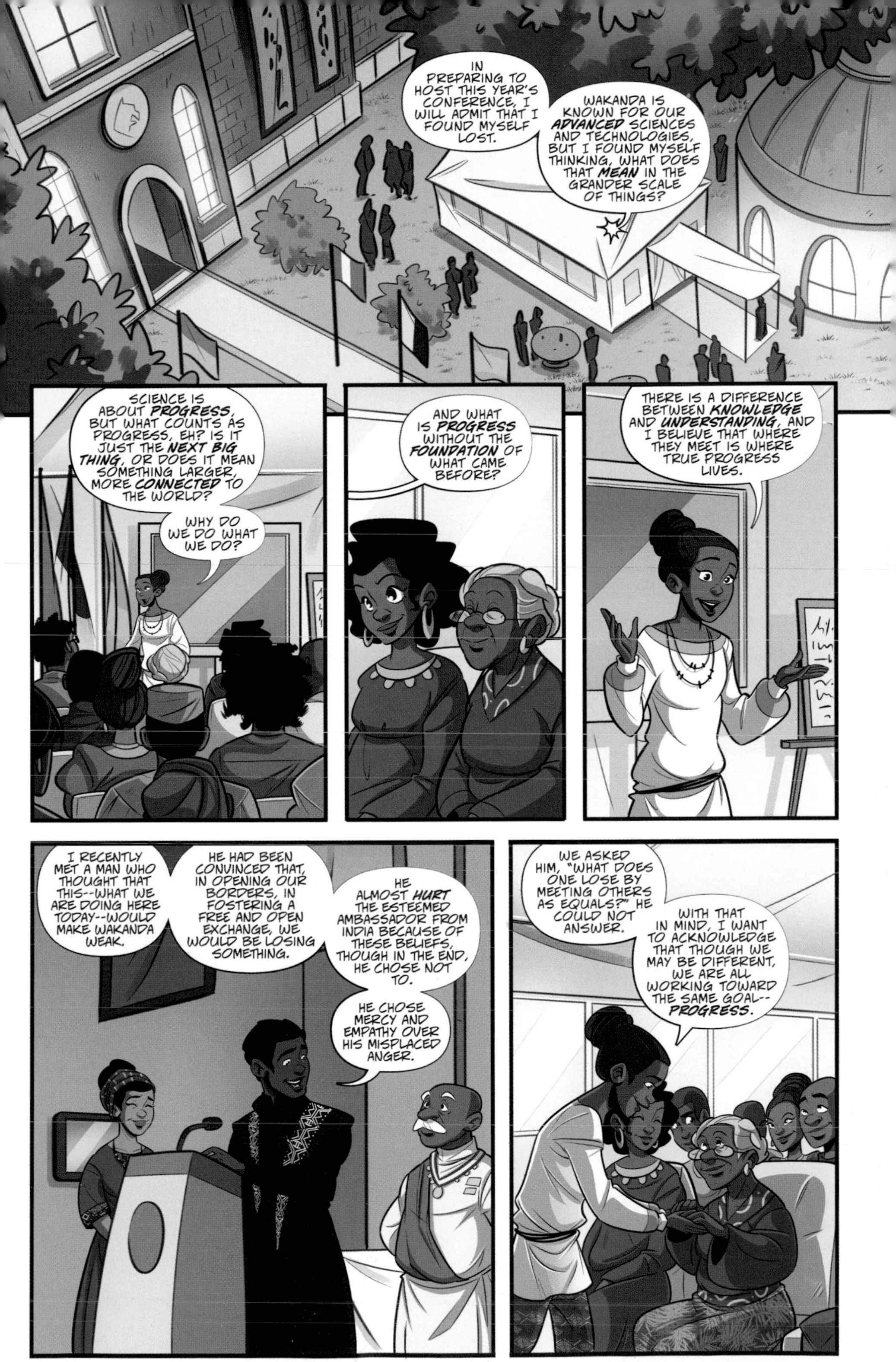
IN PREPARING TO HOST THIS YEAR'S CONFERENCE, I WILL ADMIT THAT I FOUND MYSELF LOST.
WAKANDA IS KNOWN FOR OUR ADVANCED SCIENCES AND TECHNOLOGIES, BUT I FOUND MYSELF THINKING, WHAT DOES THAT MEAN IN THE GRANDER SCALE OF THINGS?
SCIENCE IS ABOUT PROGRESS, BUT WHAT COUNTS AS PROGRESS, EH? IS IT JUST THE NEXT BIG THING, OR DOES IT MEAN SOMETHING LARGER, MORE CONNECTED TO THE WORLD?
WHY DO WE DO WHAT WE DO?
AND WHAT IS PROGRESS WITHOUT THE FOUNDATION OF WHAT CAME BEFORE?
THERE IS A DIFFERENCE BETWEEN KNOWLEDGE AND UNDERSTANDING, AND I BELIEVE THAT WHERE THEY MEET IS WHERE TRUE PROGRESS LIVES.
I RECENTLY MET A MAN WHO THOUGHT THAT THIS--WHAT WE ARE DOING HERE TODAY--WOULD MAKE WAKANDA WEAK.
HE HAD BEEN CONVINCED THAT, IN OPENING OUR BORDERS, IN FOSTERING A FREE AND OPEN EXCHANGE, WE WOULD BE LOSING SOMETHING.
HE ALMOST HURT THE ESTEEMED AMBASSADOR FROM INDIA BECAUSE OF THESE BELIEFS, THOUGH IN THE END, HE CHOSE NOT TO.
HE CHOSE MERCY AND EMPATHY OVER HIS MISPLACED ANGER.
WE ASKED HIM, "WHAT DOES ONE LOSE BY MEETING OTHERS AS EQUALS?" HE COULD NOT ANSWER.
WITH THAT IN MIND, I WANT TO ACKNOWLEDGE THAT THOUGH WE MAY BE DIFFERENT, WE ARE ALL WORKING TOWARD THE SAME GOAL--PROGRESS.

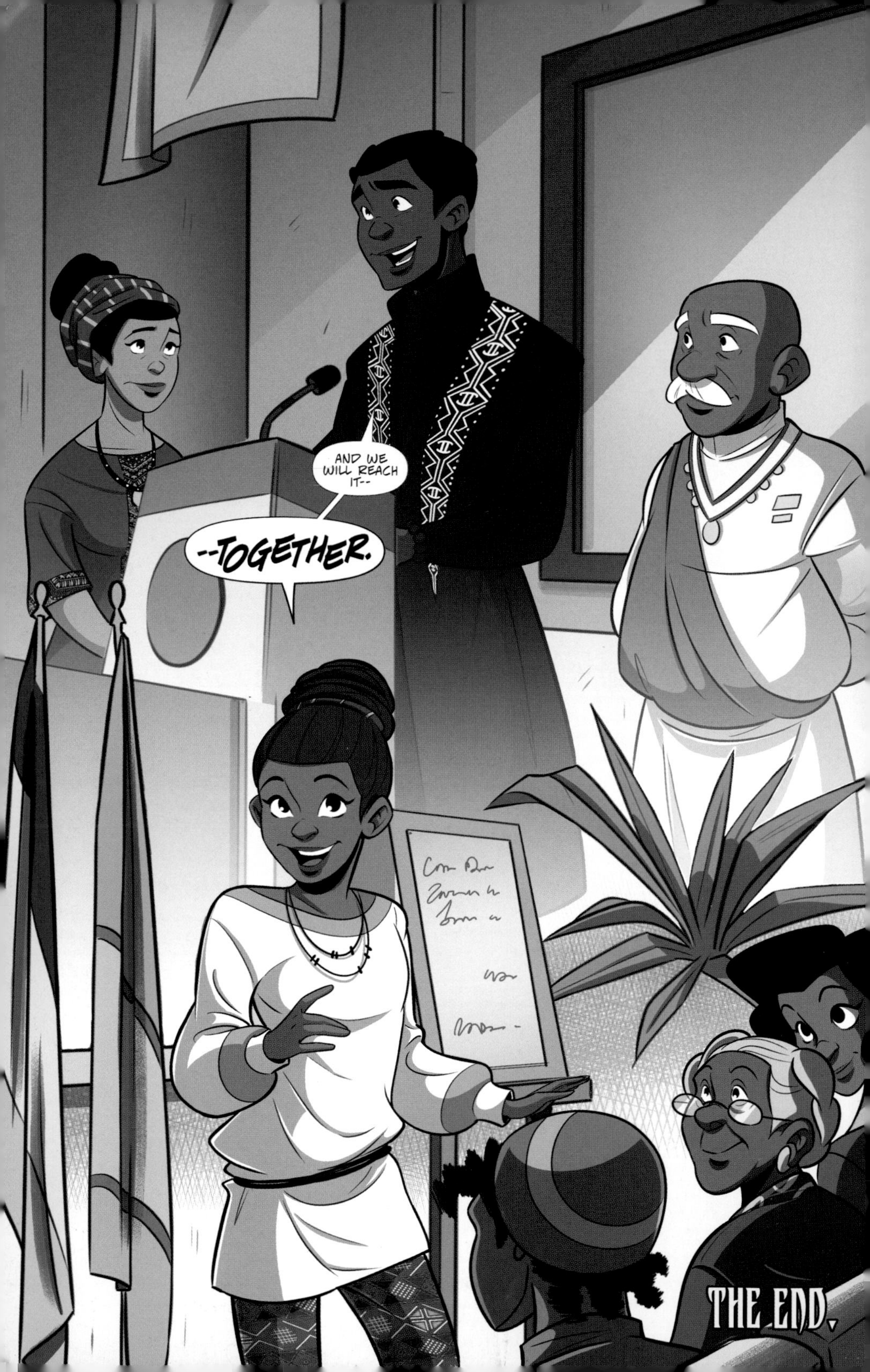
AND WE WILL REACH IT--
--TOGETHER.
THE END.

ART BY: PAULINA GANUCHEAU

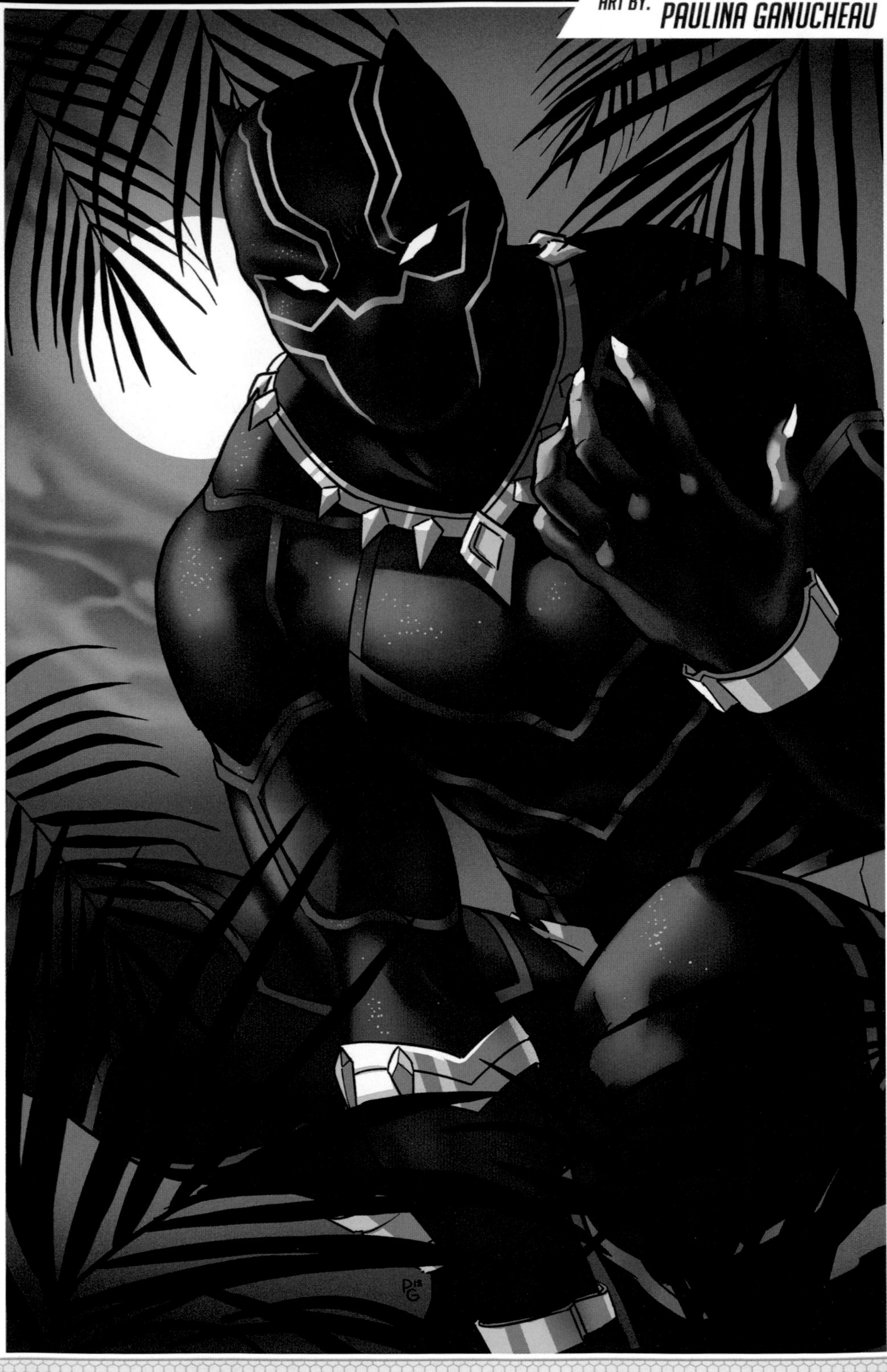

PG 18

ART BY: ASHLEY A. WOODS

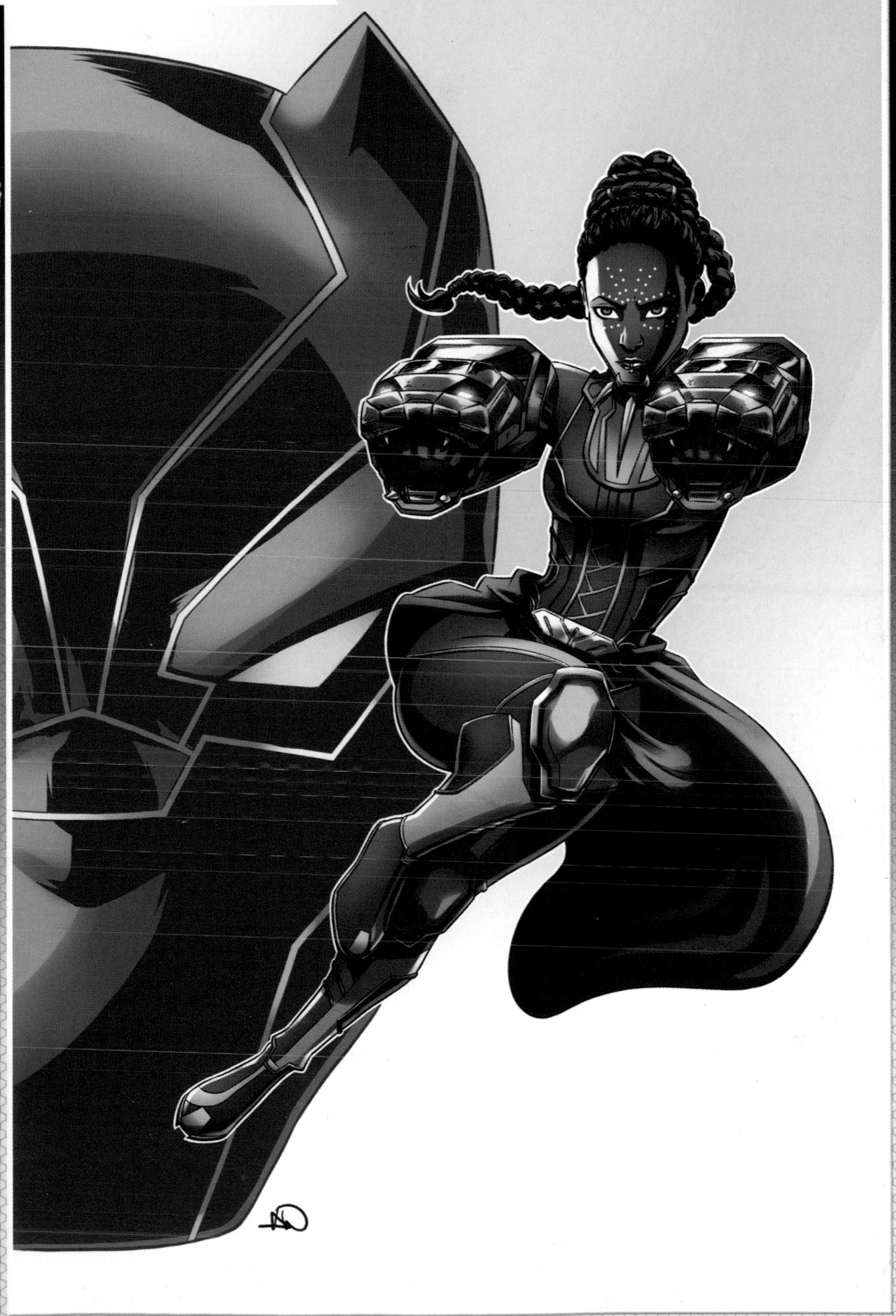

ART BY: JUAN SAMU
COLORS BY: DAVID GARCIA CRUZ

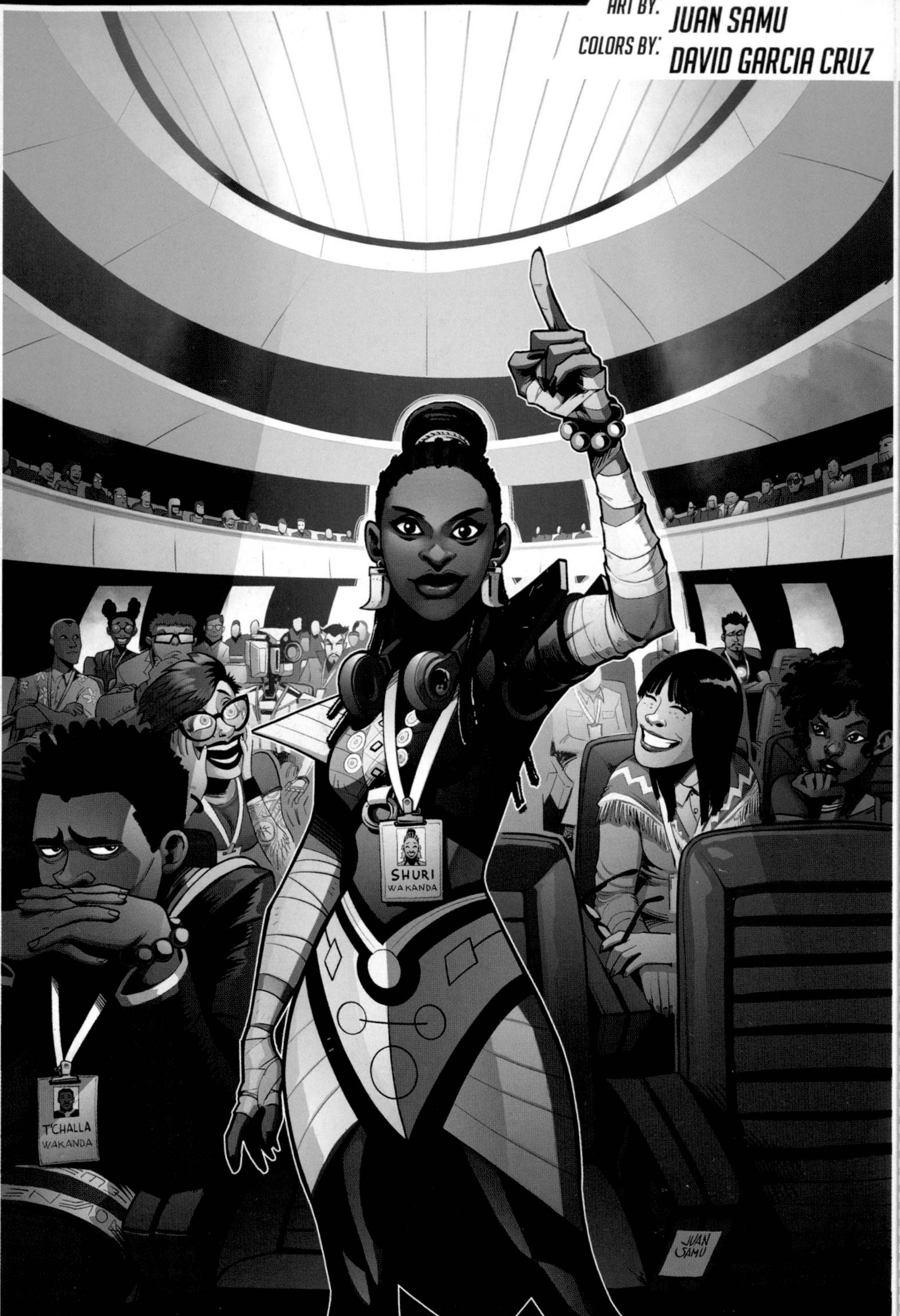
SHURI
WAKANDA
T'CHALLA
WAKANDA
JUAN SAMU